The Valley of the Giants
David Huff

David Huff Publishing
ISBN: 978-0-9988003-5-6
Card Catalogue Number:
New Jersey Heat/ David Huff
Digital distribution | 2018.
Paperback | 2018

Dedication

This book is dedicated to all of the people who believe in God when the world would have you believe in them.

"It is not what we do, but also what we do not do, for which we are accountable." — Molière

"Hold people accountable for results. If there is no accountability (consequences), people gradually lose their sense of responsibility and start blaming circumstances or other people for poor performance. When people actively participate in setting the exact standard of acceptable performance, they feel a deep sense of responsibility to get desired results." — Stephen R. Covey, The 7 Habits of Highly Effective People, page 90-92

"He doesn't know the meaning of the word fear. In fact, I just saw his grades and he doesn't know the meaning of a lot of words." — Urban Meyer, Ohio State, on one of his players

Chapter I

On a dark and stormy night as lightning flashed across a deserted valley in the Colorado mountains, a medicine man moved through the shadows near the face of the cliffs, looking for a certain tomb that held a creature, more animal than human. As he searched for the tomb the rain was starting to fall. He checked each tomb, looking for the symbols on the wall near the coffin. Finally, finding the symbols near the coffin in the last tomb that he'd been looking for, he knelt down on the ground next to the coffin and built a small fire so there would be light inside the tomb to accomplish his mission. Once this was complete, he started using the sacred sand from his medicine bag of unusual colors to draw symbols on the ground. The medicine man was angry for what the white man had done to his daughter, she had died from an overdose of drugs from her white man supplier. Being angry, he decided to get even for what had happened and he would send this giant out to find the white man and destroy him for taking his daughter from him.

As he finished drawing the symbols on the ground, he took some powder from his medicine bag and threw it on the fire. This caused the fire to smoke and burn brighter, just for a moment. He had the drug pusher's picture next to the fire so that it would be imprinted on the creatures mind. The medicine man was now watching the coffin to see if anything was happening. He started dancing around the coffin, singing the death song, and every time he went near the fire he would throw some more powder on it, causing it to burn brighter and create more smoke. After the third time of going around the coffin, the lid started moving little by little. As the medicine man watched, he smiled and continued dancing and singing. Finally, the lid flew off the coffin, landing next to the wall. The giant sat up and howled into the night. The medicine man, still smiling at what he had done, stood back in the shadows of the tomb. He now watched the creature get up out of the coffin and leave the tomb, heading out into the darkness of the night.

The medicine man left the tomb of the creature having accomplished what he had set out to do. He was unaware that the creature was still close by and that his scent had filled the nostrils of the creature, who he thought was long gone by now. The creature, turning towards the scent of the medicine man, was now following the smell of the human scent with his nose. The medicine man hearing the howl of the creature behind him, realized he was being followed by the creature and hurried as fast as his feet could carry him. Scared for his life, he was running now, trying to get away from the giant. Feeling the ground shake with each step the creature took, the medicine man now was starting to cry. Being old and not very fast, the creature caught up to him and circled the medicine man as he looked for a weak spot to attack him. The medicine man tried to run to get away, but the creature was faster and chased him across the valley till he fell down. The creature jumped on him, grabbing his head and shaking it till it came off. Prior to his dying, the medicine man realized what he had done and what was about to happen to him. He would be the creature's first meal in centuries to appease its hunger. The howl of the creature after having killed his first meal in centuries reverberated throughout the valley.

Knowing where to look for the drug pusher was easy, having the imprint of his face in his mind from the medicine man's magic made him easy to find. Walking into the area where the pusher lived, he watched and waited for the man to be alone. As he made his way onto the reservation to make another sale, the road he took was out in the middle of nowhere. The pusher had stopped his car and was outside of it, taking a leak, when the creature attacked him. Coming from out of nowhere, the pusher never saw what hit him. The creature came up from behind him and caught him off guard. Falling to the ground, he jumped up and got back into his car. As he tried to drive away, the creature reached in and grabbed him by the head and pulled him out of the open car window. The pusher was dead in less than a minute and the creature had another meal to tide him over till he needed to eat again. Moving on from there under the cover of darkness, he started to move across the valley to look for his next meal.

The next morning the reservation police found the drug pusher's car still running with only a trace of blood near the car and some big footprints nearby. Looking inside the car, they found the dealer's unsold drugs all over the floor board. The police knew that if this had been a drug heist the drugs wouldn't still be there. They didn't know what to make of it all, except that the pusher was nowhere to be found and the local Indians would have to wait for another pusher to show up with drugs to sell them. In the end the medicine man got his last wish. Killing the man that killed his daughter at the cost of his own life. The desire for vengeance sometimes comes at a very high price.

On a lonely dirt road in the middle of nowhere, a man driving his truck is on his way home for the evening. Following the old road, it was about seven thirty and the road was empty except for the man and his truck. As he is driving, the stars were out and the shadows of the trees, that line the road, cast a somewhat unfamiliar shadow on the road that played off of the headlights of the truck. He's five miles from civilization in any direction. The only sound to be heard was the radio playing country western music. He had his window down to feel the cool breeze as he listened to the music. The roar of the river next to the road was loud because of the runoff from last winter's record snowfall. He was in his own world tonight, as he has been gone for several days on a business trip to the city of Denver. He was looking forward to being home with his family, for at least a couple of days, before having to leave once more.

As he made the turn into his driveway he saw the lights were all on in his house. He say's to himself as he exits the truck, "I need to remind the kids that the power bill for electricity is already high, and that leaving all the lights on in the house isn't helping any."

He walked into the house, expecting to be greeted by his wife and kids, but they were not there to greet him as usual. He looked through the house and finding no one there, he continued on through the kitchen and into the backyard, where he saw his wife sitting on the porch swing with their daughter huddled up next to her, as well. He looked down and saw that they were both fast asleep. Smiling, he reached down and touched his wife on the shoulder to gently wake her, and as he does so she lets out a scream and starts hitting him, yelling, "Leave my daughter alone, don't you come near me!"

He grabbed her to keep from being hit again, she then realized that it was her husband. At that point she started crying, "We need to leave here now, I will not sleep here one more night. Do you hear me!?"

Holding her, he asked, "What's wrong, what's happened?"

He then looked down at his daughter and noticed that she is still asleep, and he couldn't believe that she was, especially, with all of the noise from her mother. Grabbing his daughter, he tried to wake her up. "It's no use, she won't wake up, she's in a state of shock," his wife cried out.

"From what, tell me what happened? Where's Johnny?"

The mother, crying and in between her sobs, said, pointing in the direction of the back yard, "It's our dog Sammy, he's over there. I don't know where Johnny is."

The husband, looking at his wife, puzzled, walks out to the back yard and using a flashlight from the house, he finds the dog laying on the ground dead. As he gets closer to the dog he realizes that half of the dog is gone and all that's left is the front half. The rest of the dog is nowhere to be found. As he grimaces from the sight of the blood all around the dog, he continues to search for his son around the yard. Finding nothing else that's out of place, he walked back to the porch where his wife and daughter were. Taking their daughter in his arms and leading his wife through the house to the front door, he loaded them into the truck, "You stay here, I'm going back to look for Johnny. Lock all of the doors and whatever you do don't unlock them for anyone except me, and be ready to drive if I don't come back."

As he made sure that the truck locks were engaged, he went back into the house and headed for the backyard. As he stepped into the backyard, he heard a blood curdling scream coming from out of the darkness, and it sounded very close by. As he made his way into the backyard, he starts calling for Johnny again. He heard some crying coming from behind their shed, going around he saw the boy hiding in some stacked firewood. Slowly making his way to the firewood, carefully stepping over the fallen wood, he called his name again, this time he heard the boy crying from inside the pile of wood. Finding him curled up in a ball, he grabbed him and picked him up. Holding the boy close to him, he took off running to the back of the house, going through the kitchen, and the front room, then out the front door and to the truck. The wife is watching for both of them, she sees him with Johnny, and unlocking the door for her husband, the man hands Johnny to his wife. He then goes around to the other side of the truck and jumps into the driver's seat, ready to drive them out of there. As he's leaving the driveway and turning onto the dirt road, he catches the glint of light, bouncing off of the obsidian spear point. The spear hits the side of the truck bed and a blood curdling scream is heard coming out from the darkness again. Not stopping to check it out, he shoves the truck into drive and they take off down the road. With the creature chasing after them.

As he's driving down the dirt road, he spots what looks like a giant shadow chasing him in his rearview mirror. Slowly pulling away from the shadow, they continue driving to the main highway and make their way to the bright lights of a gas station near the city, where there is civilization close by. Stopping at the gas station, he got out of the truck and found a spear buried in the side of his truck bed, stuck at a ninety-degree angle to the truck. At this point, he dialed 911 for the Douglas County Sheriff's department. Within five minutes a deputy's car pulled into the gas station, with the deputy looking at the spear in the side of the man's truck. After getting out of his car, he stood there for a moment looking at the spear. "So, what happened tonight? Have you been hunting out there in the dark?" The deputy said as he smiled, thinking it was a prank of some kind.

When the man didn't laugh, the deputy could tell he wasn't in the mood for a joke. Getting serious, the deputy started asking questions about what had happened to his truck. The man explained everything as best as he could without sounding crazy to the deputy as he continued looking at the spear.

"We need to go take a look at your place and see if we can find out who did this," said the deputy.

"If you go, you go by yourself then. I'm not going anywhere near that house tonight."

The deputy, looking at the man and his family, could tell he was looking at some scared people and wasn't sure what to do. Walking back over to his car, he called in on his police radio, "We've got and interesting situation here at Mel's gas stop, can I get some back up here please."

In a couple of minutes, two other squad cars showed up. As each of the deputies came over to look at the truck, one of them asked the deputy that had called for backup, "What's going on here?"

"I don't know what to make of this," as he pulled on the spear that was stuck in the truck. "The owner of the truck claims there's something that attacked him and his family tonight at their home and he refuses to go back out there tonight. From the looks of it, something has scared these people really bad."

"Do you think this is some kind of prank?" asked one of the deputies.

"I don't think so. You see that young girl, she hasn't moved since I got here. I think she is in some kind of shock."

"Sounds like we need to go back out there and take a look around."

At this point, all three of the deputies walk over to the man, "We need to go back out there and take a look tonight."

"Are all of you going out there? If so, I'll go with you."

All three got back into their squad cars with the man in the lead car. After turning off the state road, they drove down the dirt road, with the man of the house showing them where to go. As they pulled into the driveway, their headlights hit the house. It looked as if a tornado had touched down on the house. All three of the deputies got out of their cars, with their guns drawn and flashlights on, searching the area and finding nothing, they then started searching the ruins of the house. There was a small fire burning in the middle of the main living room. Fanning out from there, one of the deputies found a large footprint, the size he had never seen before. Calling the others over to look at it, they stood there for a moment, when they heard a blood curdling scream from up on the mountain, behind the house. All of them shined their flashlights into the darkness, not seeing anything, they looked at each other, "We need to get back to the city to report this," the senior deputy said.

The creature, seeing the flashlights near the house, started coming back down the mountain to check out where the lights were coming from. Seeing the four men standing there, he waited once more to attack. Knocking an arrow onto the bow, he waited for the right time to shoot. As he maneuvered around, he could smell the men gathered there together. Waiting until one of them was alone, he let go of his arrow, hitting one of the men in the leg.

As they were leaving the area, one of the deputy Sheriffs let out a scream in pain. Sticking in his leg was the biggest arrow that anybody had ever seen in their lives. With the help of the owner of the house, they grabbed the deputy and put him into one of the squad cars while the two deputies started to apply a tourniquet on his leg, right above the arrow, to stop the bleeding. Once this was done, one of the deputies jumped into the front seat and drove them back to the city, requesting an ambulance for the hurt deputy to meet them at the gas station. By this time, realizing he was being left behind, the man of the house jumped into the other squad car and followed right behind them. Having a once in a life time opportunity to drive a squad car he turned on the lights and the siren as he headed back into town.

The creature was unable to claim his prize when the other men came and helped the one deputy he had hit with the arrow. There were too many of them to attack, and so he stayed where he was, in the shadows waiting for them to leave. Having missed his next meal, he screamed in frustration as the deputies drove away.

The senior deputy called the Douglas County Sheriff's department, "We have an officer down and hurt!"

The Sheriff, hearing the call come in over the radio, got up from his desk and rushed over to meet them at Mel's gas stop. Seeing the hurt deputy he asked, "What happened?"

One of the two deputies told the Sheriff, "We went to check out this man's house, when we got there we found the house was completely destroyed. We then heard a blood curdling scream and the next thing we know, Smith is hit with the biggest arrow we've had ever seen."

The Sheriff walked over to the truck and saw the spear sticking in the side of it. Then looking at the arrow again, he couldn't believe the size of either one. Looking into the darkness towards the mountains, he asked himself, "Just what the hell is going on out there?"

Turning around when he heard the sirens of the ambulance, the Sheriff went with the wounded deputy to the hospital. As they rode in the ambulance, the medics gave the deputy a sedative and a pain killer for the ride to the hospital. The belt from one of the other deputies was still in place around his leg and helped in slowing the bleeding from the wound.

After arriving at the emergency room, the doctors proceeded to cut his pant leg off to get at the wound. Closing the curtain behind him, the Sheriff would have to wait for the prognosis after the doctors performed their duties. Within an hour the ER doctor came out from the behind the curtain, walking up to the Sheriff said, "He's going to make it but he won't be dancing for quite a while. It could take a month for the leg to heal up."

"How bad is it?"

"If it hadn't been for the deputies putting that tourniquet on his leg, he would have bled out. That being said, he'll recover but it's going to take some time though."

"Thanks doc, can I see him now?"

"Best wait till tomorrow, he's sedated right now."

"Until then, thanks doc for all that you did for him."

"That's why they pay us the big bucks you know."

Chapter II

As the sunlight shown through the windows in each of their offices, Jim and Julie sat behind their desks grading papers for the end of semester exams. As they did so, they were chuckling at some of the answers that were written on the exams from some of their first-year students in the basic science course in archeology. Jim liked the answer from one student where the bonus question was: Explain the theory of relativity and the answer he gave was 'It's not what you know, it's who you know, that helps in getting jobs.' Of course, it was wrong, but none the less, amusing to see the reply. Einstein would be turning over in his grave with an answer like that or maybe even laughing. The day was almost done and they were ready for the weekend to start. The grading of papers was completed by early afternoon. There were no more classes for the day and Julie was finishing the last test papers from her own class when Jim walked into her office to check if she was ready to go.

"About done with your test papers?"

"One more test, I'm beginning to think there is no hope for the human race as we now know it, based upon some of the answers on these exams."

"I know what you mean, how they ever got past high school makes me wonder if there is intelligent life on earth."

"I remember some instructor telling me one time that students are like water balloons, no matter how hard you try to form them they go back to being in the original shape they started off with."

"I wonder if that's how our teachers thought of us when we first started out in school?"

"I hope not, hey why don't we go out for dinner tonight, there is something I need to talk to you about that kind of just came up."

"Can we try Tucanos Restaurant? I've heard from some of the other faculty that it's a good place to eat and they rave about all the other types of meat they serve while you're eating from the salad bar they have there."

"What kind of food is it?"

"Brazilian Grill style food, you know fried bananas and such, and a chocolate cake they call death by chocolate, it's to die for."

Thinking for a minute Jim said, "Why not, we haven't had an adventure in quite a while."

Julie finished putting a grade on the final paper she had been looking at and then placed it on top of the other tests she had finished grading. Grabbing the rest of the papers, she got up from her desk and walked out of her office to the front of the reception area where she handed the graded tests to her student aide for her to upload the grades onto the computer.

"Just so you know, we're going to get a head start on the weekend now in case anybody needs me, I won't be back until Monday."

The student aid looked at her, "Have a nice weekend and I'll see you on Monday."

Julie and Jim left the building and walking out onto the sidewalk, they headed out to their vehicle. The sun felt good and warmed them up after being in the air-conditioned office most of the day. Getting into their Jeep, they drove to Tucanos for dinner. The atmosphere was light, and the place was spacious, and the food was excellent as usual. They would have waiters come by with meat on a skewer and slice some of it off for them to try. When they were full, they turned the wooden marker up to show red. That would show that the customer was done trying the samples of food they brought to each table.

In between dinner and desert Jim looked at Julie, "I need to talk to you about something that happened to me the other night while I was asleep."

"What was that, was it a bad dream or something?"

By now, the waitress brought them the chocolate cake with a scoop of ice cream on the side and with two spoons. Waiting for the waitress to leave before starting again, he looked at Julie, "It was something, you remember Red Hawk from the valley in Colorado?"

"How can I forget, you got shot that night and I met four giants for the first time that were alive and yet didn't exist." She shuddered when she thought about all that had happened that night in Colorado.

"Well, I saw him again the other night in my dreams."

"Why now, it's been almost two years since then?" she asked wondering.

"I don't know, just that he came to me in the dream with his three friends. I think he wants us to come back to the valley again."

"He warned us not to come back the last time we were there, are you certain about this?"

"It just feels right that we should go back to Colorado and visit the valley again."

"I wonder what's going on this time? It's lucky for us we have a couple of weeks off before the new semester starts again."

"We should be able to go in a couple of days, don't you think?"

"I see no reason why not, what about my father, should we see if he wants to go?"

"I'm not sure. I get the impression it's just us that needs to be there this time."

"Be that as it is, we probably should tell him before we leave, don't you think."

"Of course, we should just in case we don't make it back, that way he'll know where to look for us," Jim said smiling.

"Ha, ha, real funny."

The next couple of days were spent on getting ready for the trip back to the valley and after telling Professor Wainwright about their intentions of going back to the valley, he wanted to go as well, but he knew better than to go. The Professor had slipped and fallen while taking a shower and was recovering from the fall. Nothing major, just a sore back and some hurt pride. Still feeling a little shaky from it, he opted to send his good wishes and stay put for the summer to heal up.

When everything was in place, the Dean and the Professor both wished them luck and wanted a full report when they got back. Driving to the valley in their Jeep was still the best way for them to get there and it was the quickest way of driving to Colorado from Utah. Deciding to drive straight through, the eight-hour trip would start from Provo to follow the Spanish Fork Canyon over soldier's summit, then to Price, and on to Green River where they stopped to get gas and something to eat for the trip. From there they connected to interstate 70 and on to Colorado. Their next stop would be Grand Junction to refuel, from there they drove to Montrose and then on to Salida and Royal Gorge. Jim and Julie knew the trip well enough that a map wasn't needed to find their way to the Gorge. The 480-mile trip wouldn't be hard to do in one day. Staying again in Salida, they left early the next morning for their old dig site, leaving the jeep on the road at the trail head. Parking and unloading their backpacks from the Jeep they started their hike up the mountain once more. Both of them apprehensive about going into the area after being told not come back by giants. To Jim it was like stepping back in time, for his memories were still fresh in his mind about his experiences there. It's hard to forget about being shot in the leg and yet have no scar to show for it. For Julie it was like a rerun from an old monster movie that left you up at night with your emotions running high.

Stopping to take a break on the trail, Jim handed Julie his canteen of water to refresh herself, then taking a drink as well he stood up and looked the area over again for the first time, "I never thought we would be coming back here and I am wondering why now."

"It's the last place I ever thought we would be ever again."

Getting back up and readjusting their back packs, they were ready to go on. Finding the trail once more, they continued on their trip again. Making it to the old waterfall camp, they decided to spend the night there. As he looked the site over Jim said, "I don't think anybody has been here since we were here last."

"Looks that way to me too, you've got to admit that unless you know where you're going, you wouldn't think of coming this way at all."

"Yes, I believe you are right on that thought."

Jim put the tent up while Julie got the fire started as it was her favorite part of camping. After rolling their sleeping bags out inside the tent, Julie started making dinner for the both of them. The chill of the evening was starting to be felt where they were at. It actually felt good after all of the hiking they had done to get to their old camp at the waterfall. Jim had brought a fishing pole to try his luck on the river. Using some worms, he had found under a rock, he fished the pool at the base of the falls. Catching a couple of trout, he brought them back to have for breakfast tomorrow morning, after cleaning them, he put them into the cooler. Once done, Jim sat back and watched Julie as she began preparations for dinner. Noticing that she looked a little pale he asked her, "Are you feeling alright, you're looking pale?"

"I'm fine, I haven't been hiking in a while and I'm tired from it."

Jim decided not to pursue it anymore, other than to keep an eye on her from now on. He continued to eat his dinner as Julie came over and sat down beside him. The night was coming on and it was still cold in the high mountains. Wearing their coats and snuggling together, they stayed warm by the fire. In about another hour, Julie was starting to doze off as she sat there next to Jim by the fire. Jim got up and cleaned the dishes while she sat there comfortable leaning up against a big rock. He put the food away in their small ice chest, sealing it so no animal would be attracted by the smells from it. Once this was done, he reached for Julie and taking her by the hand, led her to the tent where they both crawled into their sleeping bags and went to sleep. He could see that she was still looking pale from the hike but didn't say anything about it, thinking a good night's sleep would be best for her.

The next morning Jim was wide awake, and he lay in his sleeping bag listening to noises coming from outside their tent. Slowly crawling out of his sleeping bag, he looked out of the tent to see a bear trying to get into their cooler. Cussing to himself thinking that he hadn't sealed it properly he waited and watched the bear playing with the cooler. Turning it over a couple of times not being able to open it, the bear got mad and left the camp. Getting up quickly, he grabbed the cooler and put it higher in the rocks to keep it away from the bear. By now Julie was awake from hearing the commotion of the bear, and noticing that Jim wasn't inside the tent, called out, "What's going on out there?"

"Nothing, just a bear trying to get our food out of the cooler is all."

Hearing this, Julie was up and out of the tent in one minute, dressed and ready to go. As she came out she was looking all around for the bear. Staying close to Jim the whole time. Jim could see she was scared and yelled, "Boo!"

Julie jumped about two feet in the air and screamed. When she came down she hit Jim, who was laughing at her. Looking at him she said, "That wasn't funny, you brute!"

"I'm sorry, it was meant as a joke nothing serious."

"I bet you got a kick out of that didn't you, watching your wife jump like that?"

Jim smiled, and nodded his head yes to her accusation. "You got to admit you jump pretty good for a girl your age."

"My age, what do you mean by that, you, you old timer."

Jim continued laughing at her for being such a girl, being scared and all. By now Julie grabbed a stick and started chasing him around the camp site yelling, "If I ever get my hands on you, you're going to think old and this girly girl is going to hurt you really bad by kicking your butt."

In a short amount of time both were winded from the running, both had to stop and take a break to catch their breath. Jim, recovering faster, grabbed Julie and pulled her in closer to him to kiss her while he was still laughing at her. Julie took her stick and hit him in the backside to let him know she was still upset with his trick and calling her old. In a minute still kissing, Julie dropped the stick and Jim quit laughing. Both stood there for a moment and breaking their kiss, he said, "what's for breakfast, sweetheart?"

"Is that all you think about is food?"

"Well it is hard to get along without it, and all this running around has made me kind of hungry."

"How would you like your eggs raw or raw?"

"I think I'll have my eggs raw, if you don't mind."

Julie went about making breakfast as Jim looked around for the fish he had caught the night before. Not finding them he looked at Julie, "Well the bear got the fish and all we got were the bones."

"No wonder the bear was here this morning, he smelled the fish you caught."

"Some bears have all of the luck."

After the breakfast of eggs and hotdogs was over, Jim put the gear back into their packs and had everything ready to go for the hike. Julie, looking a little paler than the day before, excused herself and went back up the trail into the brush to throw up. Jim could hear her and waited for her to come back down the trail, "What's wrong, are you alright Julie?"

"Something I must of ate this morning, didn't agree with me, is all."

Starting their hike back on the trail to the valley, Jim made sure the going was slow for Julie just in case she was still sick. In a while, Julie passed Jim on the trail, "You are such a slow poke."

Jim was confused by this sudden burst of energy from Julie, and was now trying to keep up with her on the trail. In what seemed like minutes, they arrived at the boulder. Getting up onto it, they looked over the valley. Standing there, looking once more over the valley, each deep in their own thoughts, wondering if they had done the right thing by coming back to the valley. Only time would tell and hopefully they wouldn't get hurt in the process.

Slowly making their way down into the valley, everything looked the same as before. Nothing seemed out of place since the last time being there. Finding the stairs and climbing to the top level, they set up camp and waited to see what would happen next.

In the mean time while they waited, Julie built another fire just in case they would be there overnight, while Jim went in search of more firewood.

Chapter III

The Douglas County Sheriff's department Sheriff and his deputies, were out the next morning looking at the house, or what was left of it. The owner was with them and a team of forensics personnel as well. The Sheriff looked at the owner of the house, "I hope you have good home owner's insurance."

"I do, I just don't know what to file the claim under."

The Sheriff smiled at the owner, "Better you than me," being serious, he continued, "Personally, I think you and your family are really lucky to have not been killed by whoever or whatever did this."

They found the squad car in pieces, slammed up against a tree in the road. The Sheriff didn't know what to make of the mess of the house or the squad car. One of the deputies, searching the area, found some footprints near the front of the house. Calling the Sheriff over to show him the tracks, he looked at them and had his forensics team get plaster molds of the tracks. All the foot prints were huge and human shaped, at least thirty-eight inches long and fifteen inches wide. Another thing that was different besides the size of the foot print, was that they had imprints of six toes on each foot.

They also found what was left of the dog in the back yard and footprints around the carcass. One of the other deputies, who had been searching outside the house perimeter, found a trail that led up into the mountains behind the house. The Sheriff debated about following it, especially, if it took them into the evening hours. Calling his office, he asked that the dispatcher have the secretary call Bill Mortenson to come out with his dogs and follow the trail. The dispatcher passed the word on to the secretary, and within five minutes dispatch called the Sheriff back, "Bill will be out there shortly with his dogs."

Thanking dispatch, he also asked the radio operator to have his secretary call the university in Fort Collins and get hold of the biology department to send a biologist, if possible, to come down to look at the footprints they had found. Again, five minutes later, dispatch called back on the radio saying it would be some time before the university could send someone out to look at the footprints, claiming it was finals week. By now, one of the deputies had followed the trail up the mountain a short distance and lost sight of it in the brush and timber. Coming back down to the Sheriff, the deputy said, "It looks as if whoever it was that made these footprints made no attempt to cover their trail up on the mountain."

"That's good, Bill will be here with his hounds to follow the trail up there to see where it goes and hopefully maybe he can find the answer to our questions. Besides, if he's as big as I think he is, I don't think he's worried about being caught."

Bill was as good a tracker as anybody they had in the county, he had lived here for years and he knew these woods like the back of his hand. He was from way back, and was used as a guide to hunt cougar and bear by hunters who paid for these kinds of hunts. He was also used, as needed, to find men and lost children in the woods. He was known throughout the state for having the best tracking dogs, all coon hounds, which he had trained himself for nearly two years. When things got lost, the Sheriff knew Bill and his hounds could find a needle in a haystack anywhere and anytime. He would give the dogs a smell from a piece of cloth or anything with what they were tracking, and Bill would release the hounds to find the owner of the smell.

During the day or night, you could hear the hounds howling as they followed the scent of the trail. The howls from the hounds would change once they found their quarry, that's how Bill knew they had found what they were looking for.

All the Sheriff could do now was wait on Bill to show up with his hounds. In about an hour Bill pulled up in his truck with the dog cages on the back of his flatbed. Through the holes of the dog cages you could hear the coon hounds baying, all wanting to get out of their cages and start tracking.

Getting out of the truck and walking over to the Sheriff, shaking hands with him, he asked "What you got?"

"Damned if I know Bill, for all I know it could be the Jolly Green Giant. Let me show you what I mean."

Taking Bill over to show him the footprints, Bill bent down to look at them and shook his head, "You might be right about the Jolly Green Giant. I've never seen anything like this before."

"Do you think you can track them back to where they came from?"

"I'm pretty sure I can, the problem is what do I do about it if I find it? I sure as hell don't want to run into this guy without some kind of backup."

"I agree with you, I can give you a couple of deputies to take with you, will that be enough for you?"

"Do you happen to have an extra RPG (rocket propelled grenade) I could use? You know, just in case," Bill said smiling as he went to get his dogs out of their cages.

Bill pulled his hounds out of their cages from the back of his truck and attached their leashes on them. Leading the dogs to the tracks, he let each of the dogs smell the tracks and once they got the scent he released them and let them go up the mountain. The Sheriff looked at two of his deputies and pointed to the mountain, nodding their heads they went with Bill to follow the dogs. As they climbed the mountain you could hear the dogs baying as they followed the scent. The deputies and Bill were having a hard time following the dogs due to the uphill terrain of the mountain, listening to the dogs was their only way of knowing which way to go, and staying on the trail. Within an hour the dogs quit howling, and all was quiet. Bill wasn't quite sure what to make of this and was now starting to get worried about his dogs.

Working their way up the mountain, they could follow the tracks of, not only the dogs, but what they were after as well. Bill was still concerned that he couldn't hear the dogs anymore and kept moving up the mountain. The two deputies were a little slower going up the mountain, but they could tell something was wrong as they couldn't hear the dogs anymore either. Climbing as fast as they could go, they found Bill sitting on a tree stump on the ridge of the mountain resting a minute to catch his breath. When they had caught up to him, Bill pointed at the ground, "Look, blood over there and here too."

The deputies, after catching their breath, chambered their weapons and had them ready just in case and started moving and looking the area over. One of them standing by a tree, found some blood next to it. Looking around, he couldn't see where it originated from. Taking his hat off he wiped the sweat from his face, that's when he felt something hit his cheek. Rubbing it off his cheek he looked at his hand, seeing that it was red, looked up and stepped back, "Hey Bill, you need to come over and take a look at this."

Bill came over and saw the deputy looking up into the tree, he could see what looked like the body of an animal hanging on one of the branches. Recognizing it as one of his dogs he started looking around to find the other dog. The second deputy came over, and climbing up the tree, was able to lower the dog to the ground. Bill came back with his other dog, carrying it in his arms. Both dogs were dead. Laying them down next to each other, Bill was in tears from losing both of them. At this point, all three of them heard a scream, like it was from a mountain lion, but louder and more powerful.

Looking around the area, they decided to go and see where the scream came from to try and figure out what it was that could throw a dog into a forty-foot tree. Following the noise, they cleared the crest of the mountain and started down the other side, looking for the noise and where it was coming from. Going from tree to tree using them as cover, Bill was following the second deputy as they continued down the mountain following the trail. The first deputy, carrying a shotgun with him, had taken the lead and was working his way down the mountain when he saw the cave. Motioning with his hand for the other two, they came up to where he was standing behind the tree. Looking into the cave and not seeing anything, the lead deputy decided to light up the cave. Taking some kindling wood from off the ground and bunching it together in a kerchief, he lit the kindling on fire and threw it into the cave. As he did this, he made his way to the side of the cave opening, waiting to see what would happen next. The second deputy, who had covered the first deputy as he built the fire moved over to the side of the cave, then moved closer to the front of the cave. Waiting to see what would happen, the fire grew bigger and began to light up the cave inside. The deputy, standing in front of the cave with Bill, could see clearly that there was nothing inside the cave. Moving out into the open, the deputy didn't see the arrow that hit him in the shoulder. Screaming in pain, the deputy went down, with Bill catching him before he hit the ground. The deputy at the mouth of the cave seeing his cohort get hit with the arrow, waited for whoever shot his partner to show. Looking around and seeing a big shadow in the trees, he fired his shotgun into it. The blast of the 12-gauge double odd buck hit its target and the creature made a noise of pain from being hit. This time Bill grabbed the deputy's gun and started firing into the trees. The first deputy fired his shotgun again, hitting the creature again, the howling of the creature could be heard all over the canyon. By now the creature took off into the brush and ran along the ridge and was gone. Bill called out to the deputy, "We need to get your partner down off the mountain before he bleeds out on us and dies."

Tying a tourniquet on his arm to stop the bleeding, they helped the wounded deputy climb back over the ridge and down the mountain to where the Sheriff's car was. Upon arriving, the Sheriff called for an ambulance. When the hurt deputy was taken off of the mountain the Sheriff was now getting pretty upset about losing two deputies and a squad car and still not knowing what it was that did the damage. He walked over to Bill, who sat there in silence by his truck, "What happened up there?"

"I don't really know Sheriff, all I know is I found one of my dog's dead up in a tree, 40 feet up, and the other one dead on the trail. When we tracked the creature, we thought he was in a cave that we had found on the other side of the ridge. Lighting it up with some fire, we realized he wasn't in there. A minute later the deputy gets hit by an arrow in the shoulder and the other deputy started firing his shotgun into a group of trees next to the cave, hitting the creature twice. I grabbed the hurt deputy's gun and started firing into the trees as well. When we went to check it out, the creature was gone. Evidently, he took off onto the other side of the ridge. That's when we decided to bring your hurt deputy back down the mountain before he died."

"You expect me to believe that you shot and hit the creature with your gun and a shotgun and you couldn't find the body anywhere?"

"Frankly Sheriff, I don't care what you believe, all I know is that my two dogs are dead, and you got a wounded deputy with an arrow sticking out of him. You believe what you want. The fact is, you go up on the mountain and see if you can find the creature yourself."

"I think you're afraid to go back up there again, Bill."

"You damn right I am, and if you had any sense you would be too as well. Is there anything else I can do for you Sheriff?"

The Sheriff, shocked by Bill's answer, just stood there for a moment, speechless at Bill's reply. Shaking his head, no, "You can go now."

"Thanks Sheriff," he said sarcastically, as he walked to the cab of his truck and got in. "You owe me two dogs, Sheriff, and I <u>will</u> collect from you," he said as he was driving off.

The Sheriff stood there not knowing what to do now. He knew Bill well enough to know that nothing would scare him this bad. He started thinking to himself, "*Maybe this is bigger than my men can handle alone, after seeing Bill's reaction makes me think it might be time to call in some favors for some help from my friends in law enforcement. But who's going to believe me when I tell them what we're hunting.*"

Driving off the mountain, thinking about his two deputies, he decided to go visit them to see if they had any information that would help them in tracking the creature.

Chapter IV

The creature was a giant that looked like a man, he stood 15 feet tall, had six fingers, six toes, and a double set of teeth in its mouth, weighing about eleven hundred pounds. In all other aspects, he looked like a man, but his thinking process hadn't reach that full capability yet. He was more animal than human and was considered a freak by everyone that saw him. Being a cannibal, he was used to eating the smaller men if he could catch them. But anything that was a mammal was fair game for him, as well, to eat. His capability to smell out the warm-blooded animals made him good at surviving. The last thing he remembered was being kept in a cave, where the others would feed him and take care of him. He didn't like the cage, but they treated him good there and he never worried about being hungry like he has to now.

The men who had shot him scared him more than hurt him. Being a healer, which meant he could recover quickly from any wound he received, meant it would only take an hour to recover from the wounds he received from the shotgun and the other thing that kept flashing at him, those stung but really didn't do anything to him. Being scared by the man with the stick in his hand and feeling pain, he ran off not knowing what to do. He had been scared like this once before when he had been inside another cave, when they lit the cave on fire many years ago. Watching the man light up his cave with fire again forced him into the stand of trees. Preferring to hide than attack, he waited for the right time to make his move. When he saw the man come out from behind the tree, he shot his arrow at him hoping to eat him. He didn't expect the others to attack him with their fire sticks.

Hiding now from the men, he waited until dark to look for food, if only they hadn't removed the animal from the tree he could've eaten that and been full for the night. In the creature's mind he knew he needed to go find food to survive. Looking around and sniffing the air, he knew there were other animals in the woods he could eat, but the taste of man he craved and missed the most. Looking around and trying to catch the scent of man in the woods he didn't find any. He would continue hunting for them for his survival. Staying on the shady side of the ridge, he moved downhill looking for any signs of man.

Chapter V

Having accomplished setting up their camp, and still having plenty of daylight left, they decided to go exploring the tombs on the first level below their campsite. Going into each one of them and checking to see that each of them was secure, they didn't find anything out of place with the exception of the one that had been setup as a cage for the giant creature that they had found inside. Somebody had removed the lid of the coffin and the body from its tomb. In fact, the coffin had been vandalized by something or someone. Looking around they couldn't see anything else missing. Jim noticed that the cover for the coffin had been pushed off and was laying on the ground about five feet away. He asked himself, "Why would anyone mess with only one of the tombs and why this one? What made this one more interesting than the others in their tombs?"

Going back over in his mind, he remembered the skull of this one having two sets of teeth along with six fingers and six toes. This giant was different from the others, standing larger than the other giants that lay in their own coffins. Jim wondered how he was able to get free from the coffin and wondered if he was alive now or if someone had taken the bones for their own purpose. None of this made sense as he stood there inside the tomb, but then again neither did having a burial ground for giants either.

As Jim continued looking in the tomb, he found some painted sand on the ground next to the coffin with the remains of a fire near it, as well. Someone had been in here recently and from the looks of it, it happened to be an Indian. Or someone who knew about the Indian ways. Calling Julie over to take a look at the sand painting on the floor of the cave, plus the remains of the fire he asked, "What do you make of this?"

Julie knelt down and looked at the sand painting on the ground and then the fire place, "I think were not alone out here, I think someone else knew about this valley as well."

Jim stepped out of the cave and finding the footprints of the giant, he followed them across the valley floor. Julie was right behind him looking for anything that might show the location of the creature they were following. Jim laughed as he walked the valley floor, "Who in their right mind would be following a giant who eats people to find out where he went?"

After a few minutes he stopped, telling Julie not to move or look at where he was going. He saw what was left of the medicine man's remains. Of course, there was blood everywhere around him, but all that was recognizable was his feet.

"What is it, what do you see?" Julie asked.

"A body of a man or what's left of it."

Julie didn't wait any longer, walking over to see for herself and turning away when she saw what was left of the man. Jim looking a little closer found the remains of some Levi material on one of the bushes. His two hands were found in some sagebrush not too far away, as Jim made a wide arc searching around the scene, thinking out loud, "We need to call the law in on this one before we go any further."

Julie was way ahead of him and was calling on the cell phone when Red Hawk appeared to them. Catching them both off guard, they stopped what they were doing and waited to hear from Red Hawk. Looking at both of them and with a smile he said, "I'm glad you're here."

"I wasn't sure you would be," Jim replied.

"As you can see we have a problem out here, that was a medicine man who brought the creature to life that was inside the cave you just came from."

"Is this the one that likes to eat humans for dinner?" Julie asking this time.

"Yes, as a matter of fact he does, however, he has eaten only one human so far that we know of," looking and pointing at the remains of the medicine man on the desert floor.

"How are we supposed to stop him from killing anymore people?" Jim asked.

"That's easy, you two are the bait for him," Red Hawk chuckled.

"Somehow, I think this is a bad idea for us. What are we supposed to do to accomplish that?"

"Bring him back here and we'll do the rest once you get him here."

"Where is he now?" Julie asked.

"Don't worry about that, he'll find you. Remember this valley is still not to be known about yet," Red Hawk said and then disappeared.

"Oh great, we got to let a creature that is a cannibal find us, so we bring him back here to put him back in his coffin, and we can't tell anyone about it to get the help we need to do this," Jim said as he sat down on a tree stump.

"Well, one thing for sure, we are having the time of our lives out here, aren't we?"

As they continued to follow the tracks, they started heading in a direction that was taking them in a more northeasterly direction from where they had started. Realizing this, they headed back to their camp and repacked their gear before heading out to find the trail again. This time going in the direction of the creature, they quickly found his trail and started following it. Jim, thinking about their conversation with Red Hawk, said out loud, "You know he didn't say we couldn't call your dad or the Dean."

"No, he didn't, did he? Besides they already know about the valley."

Julie took her cell phone out and tried calling her dad, waiting for the ring tone, looking at her cell phone said, "Rats, we have no bars out here, and we don't have any water either," she chuckled

Jim laughed, "Well, we need to keep trying as we follow the trail."

As they continued to follow the footprints left by the creature, Jim could tell they were climbing and the trail wasn't as clear as it once was. Occasionally stopping to get their bearings, Jim could tell Julie was getting tired. Stopping for her to catch her breath made it easier for her as they made their ascent up the mountain. Sitting on top of the mountain, Julie was able to get a call out to her father to explain what was going on. Professor Wainwright said he would meet them at their Jeep near the Gorge. Turning around, they headed back down to the valley. Going down the mountain was easier than climbing, therefore they made good time going back to the cliffs. Julie had Jim set up their camp again while she cooked their dinner. This time there was plenty of food and Julie took most of it to eat for herself. Jim watched as she devoured everything on her plate, wondering if she was the creature herself, "You aren't hungry, are you?"

"I don't know, it's just all of a sudden I'm famished since we started that hike and everything."

"Remind me not to get in your way while eating, I could lose a hand in there."

Julie turned red from his joke, not saying anything, she got up to clean the dishes. Jim looked out into the valley as he sat there thinking about what Red Hawk had said, and trying to come up with a plan on how to get the creature back to the valley. When Julie was done with cleaning the dishes, she came over and sat down next to him. As they sat in silence looking at the stars and the valley below, she said, "I really don't know why I'm so hungry lately or for that matter being so sick. I don't understand any of this at all."

"How are you feeling now?"

"I feel fine, but this morning my stomach was queasy, and I didn't want to eat anything, thinking I would throw it up again. I don't understand this at all."

"Well, as long as you feel fine now, I'm sure it will go away soon."

"I hope so, we got a lot to accomplish here, and I can't be under the weather trying to get that creature back here."

"Not to worry, we'll get through this."

Spending another night there, they left the following morning back to the Jeep. As they waited for Julies dad to show up, they sat in the jeep listening to the news on the radio. At one-point Jim turned up the radio as he heard the news announcer saying, "A house that's located in the foothills outside of Castlerock has been destroyed and several animals have been killed by an unknown creature that has also been responsible for injuring two deputies when they went after whatever it was that killed a tracker's dogs."

Jim looked at Julie, "I think they found our friend."

"Did it say where this all happened in the report?"

"South of Denver, up in the mountains near a small town."

Julie called her dad on the cell phone, "Instead of meeting us here in the gorge meet us in Colorado Springs, near Manitou Springs at a place called 'Friends Coffee and Espresso. We'll be sitting in the patio area when you show up."

The Professor acknowledged the location, "We'll be there in a couple of hours."

Jim and Julie still had another hour to drive to get there themselves. Getting to Interstate 25, they drove through Colorado Springs and took State Route 24 and arrived there in about 45 minutes. Finding the coffee shop, the sat down and ordered lunch. While they waited for Julie's dad they ate their lunch in the patio area, as it was still nice and cool for the beginning of the summer. Eventually, Professor Wainwright showed up with the Dean in tow. Jim and Julie stood up and hugged them both. Looking surprised that the Dean was there, Jim asked, "Dean, what made you decide to come a long on the trip?"

"I remember the fun we had last time we were in Colorado. Did you think I would want to miss out on all of the fun on this trip?"

"You may wish you had, Dean," Julie said.

The waitress was there in seconds asking, "What would you two like to order?"

"A couple of sandwiches and a couple drinks," The Dean said, the Professor nodded in agreement.

"Is that to stay or go?" The waitress asked.

Looking at Jim, he said, "To go."

The Professor and the Dean sat and listened to Jim as the waitress hustled off to get the food. He told them about what they had found in the valley with the one of the coffins being opened by a medicine man and finding his remains. He also told them about the radio report and how the creature was free and roaming the countryside. As they listened the Professor asked, "Do you have an idea where it might be?"

"No not really, but we have heard reports about some vandalism happening just south of Denver, in the mountains in a small town called Castlerock, not too far from here. That's why we had you meet us here instead of in the valley."

"Do you think there is a connection?" the Dean asked.

"We're not sure, but it's the best lead we have right now," Julie continued, "We want to drive to where all of this took place and talk to the police to find out more about it."

By now the waitress had the sandwiches and drinks ready for them. They paid for their food and left the café. The Professor, grabbing the sacks of food, carried them out to the truck and called out, "We'll follow you."

Jim waved his hand in agreement as he got into their Jeep and started the engine. Julie, looking at a local map of the area said, "Do you realize they have cliff dwellings not too far from here? It's called Manitou cliff dwellings."

"Yes, I saw that on the map as well. I studied it while you were in the restroom, the ruins of the ancient Indian site are too new and too small for our friends that we know of."

"I wonder if the Indians ancestors were the ones that killed the creature's friends?"

"Hard to say without looking into it. Maybe the creatures ate the Indians and that's why they aren't around anymore."

Julie, gave him a look, "Aren't you just a bundle of sunshine today."

"Sometimes, I crack myself up," Jim laughed.

"Just drive."

Chapter VI

The Douglas County Sheriff was sitting in his office in Castlerock, waiting for the biologist to call on him so that he could explain what they had seen out there at the house, and also on the mountain. The Sheriff's secretary knocked on his door and entered, "There is a man here to see you, he says he's from the university up north."

The Sheriff stood up and moved from around his desk, "Kindly show him in would you."

In a second the biologist was walking through the Sheriff's door and shook hands with the Sheriff, "My name is Professor Davis from Colorado State University, I hear you have some interesting things to show me."

"I sure do, and frankly I hope you can help us with this."

Having Professor Davis sit down in one of the chairs, the Sheriff told him about what had happened to two of his deputies, the family home, and squad car. As he explained, he showed the pictures of all the damage done, to the Professor. The Sheriff saved the picture of the footprints and casts for last. When Professor

Davis saw the footprints and the cast of them, he hung onto the picture the longest of them all. Looking at the Sheriff he asked, "Do you have any idea what this is from?"

"All we know at this point is that it's big and carries a spear and shoots arrows. I've got two deputies in the hospital right now recovering from the arrows that were shot at them. We were hoping you could tell us about it."

The Professor looked at the pictures of the spear and arrows and then again at the footprints. Leaning back into his chair and thinking for a moment, he looked at the Sheriff, "I don't even know where to start on this. As I remember from my reading on the subject of giants years ago, there were pictures showing footprints like these that had fossilized, with the people who had found them taking pictures showing their feet inside the footprints."

"Are you serious about this?" Looking at the biology professor, wondering if he was a nut.

"Yes, I am. The problem is, that I'm not sure that it's not all a hoax and I'm not sure what to tell you about this. This is the first time I've actually seen something like this in my life. To be honest with you, I'm still not sure I believe what I'm looking at."

The creature moved through the forest, on the run, looking for something to eat. Catching a deer, he devoured part of it within minutes, carrying the rest of the carcass with him, eating just long enough to satisfy his hunger before moving on. To the creature, the surrounding area was familiar yet different from what he had remembered. This was his old stomping grounds and in that sense, everything was as he remembered, but at the same time he had never seen cars or trucks before or, for that matter, what the deputy had used against him on the other mountain. This was puzzling to him and he wasn't sure what to do or think about it all. All he knew was that he had to be careful and not get caught and put in that cage again. His instinct to survive was paramount in his mind and through his life he would carry out this by destroying anything and everything that got in his way. Hiding in the shadows in a group of trees during the day made it easier for him to move without being seen. The cave would have been nice to stay in, but with the fire in it still burning, it was no good to him anymore.

As he waited in the shadows, a grizzly bear smelling the air caught the scent of the deer on the creature, and being hungry decided to follow the scent. It was easy to find the trail, the blood from the deer was all along the path that the creature had taken. And seeing him in the trees, stood on his hind legs and growled at him. The creature had seen bears before but not the size of this one. This one was as tall as he was and not afraid to go after him. Having lost his spear and having no more arrows as weapons, this fight would have to be hand to paw between the two of them. The creature came out of the shadows and let out a scream, challenging the bear. The grizzly stood his ground and growled back at the creature. Neither one of was afraid, each was a master of the forest in their own right. Right now, the battle was for supremacy to be king in this forest. Each standing their ground and not giving an inch, the creature charged first at the bear. The bear swung his right front paw at the creature, hitting him in the chest and raking him with his claws. Using his teeth, he caught the creature on the shoulder, and biting deep, the creature screamed in pain. Hitting the bear in the head with his other hand, the bear let go of his shoulder. The creature grabbed the bear by the head and was trying to wrap his arm around the head, all the while the bear was using his claws on the back of the creature making the wounds deep, and the creature was bleeding from them. The bear was in a headlock by the creature and was being hit in the face. The bear stood up on his hind legs, one more time, lifting the creature off the ground causing the creature to let go of him. Swiping at him again with his claws, the creature was raked across the back once more, this time tearing the flesh to the bone. The bear had lost an eye and was bleeding from it. Both were hurt by now and neither wanted to continue the fight. Backing away from each other, the bear growled again, while the creature howled out, as well. The creature would need time to heal from the bears claws and bites, the bear had never fought anything like this before and wasn't sure what to do. Both of them backed away from each other and stood their ground, while each of them continued to growl at the other before moving on. The bear would have to look for his own food and the creature would need time to heal from the battle. The creature might have considered the thought that he had won the fight, but he was in too much pain to consider it right now. The creature lay back in the shadows, waiting for his body to heal itself once more. It would be some time before he would move again from where he was, having the deer carcass to eat would have to do for food.

Watching all of this, was a mountain lion, sitting in a tree smelling the deer as well. The cat moved from its perch and came down to see if it could get the deer carcass. Moving closer to the helpless creature he came up and growled at the creature, at this point all the creature could do was lay there. Taking the deer carcass, the cat dragged it away and now the creature had nothing to eat. He was lucky that the mountain lion wanted only the deer. Closing his eyes, he was safe for the moment.

Jim and Julie drove to the Douglas County Sheriff's office with the Dean and Professor Wainwright following them. Reaching the secretary first, Jim spoke for the four of them and asked to speak to the Sheriff about the incidents dealing with the house and the car. The Sheriff was in no mood for visitors, since the biologist left with no answers but wild stories for the Sheriff. The secretary asked who they were, they gave their names and said also that they were professors in archeology from Brigham Young University. The secretary went into the Sheriff's office, "Some professors from some university in Utah are here to see you."

The Sheriff thought for a moment, and looked at his secretary, "Oh, what the hell, why not have them come in."

When all four of them showed up, the Sheriff had the secretary bring in some extra chairs to accommodate everyone in the room. When everyone was finally seated the Sheriff said, "Now what can I do for all of you."

Jim spoke first, "I think we can help solve your mystery about the house. Can we see your pictures please?"

Handing the pictures over to the four of them, each of them looked at them and then passed them around, handing them back to the Sheriff after they were done.

"I think what you have here is a giant man, that is about twelve feet tall and has six toes and six fingers," Jim said, as he looked at the Sheriff.

"How did you know about the six toes, we never let that out in our broadcast."

"Let's just say for the sake of not causing an argument, we have seen this giant for the time being, and have we got a story for you."

The Sheriff was all ears at this point, as Jim told the story of giants and how they existed three thousand years ago. By now the Dean and Professor Wainwright showed him pictures of giant skeletons being buried in graves that were found by normal people everywhere. The Sheriff, looking at Jim asked, "What kind of water have you been drinking that you expect me to believe all of this."

"Don't take our word for it, just ask yourself about the size of the spear and the arrows that you've found."

"Let's just say I believe you, which I don't, how do we stop this giant?"

Jim sat back and then slowly said, "Well first of all, you can't kill it and second, you put any man or men against it, the giant will try and kill them to eat them. You see, he's a cannibal."

"Frankly, were surprised that no one else has been eaten by this giant," Professor Wainwright said.

"Your deputies were lucky that they had backup when they got hurt, otherwise, they would be dead," Julie added.

The Sheriff was trying not to believe any of what he was being told. Yet, here was an answer to his questions from people who came from Utah. And it coincided with the biology professor from up north.

"So how do you plan to stop him?"

"Well, we need to take him back from where he came from and put him back where he will be safe, and you and your town will be safe as well."

"You still haven't answered my question, professors."

"We need him to think we are his next meal and lead him back to the valley."

"You're kidding me, right?"

"I wish we were, but we are not kidding you."

The Sheriff thought about all that he had heard, and seeing that the professors were dead serious said, "I don't know what or who you think I am but this is the biggest bunch of malarkey I've ever heard and if you ever try to come back in here again, I'll lock you up for sure. Do you hear me, now get out of my office and don't ever come back here again?"

All of the team got up and walked out of the office. Jim turned and looked at him, "You're making a big mistake Sheriff. We really are here trying to help you."

"Get out of my office now!" quickly closing his door. He sat back down at his desk, grabbed the pictures and threw them across the room shaking his head and mumbling, "Three thousand year old giants with six fingers and toes."

As they left the Sheriff's office and went back out to the street they all stood there looking at each other, "I thought that went rather well, didn't you all," Julie said.

"Well what do we do now?" asked the Dean, a bit perplexed now.

"That's easy, we need to find the creature on our own," Professor Wainwright said.

"Yep, that's what we do now, the question is where do we look for him?" Jim added.

Thinking about their next move and not knowing where to go, the Dean said, "The way we find him is, we turn on the radio and listen to the local radio station for anything happening out of the ordinary."

"Let's find a hotel or motel and wait in the rooms for the local news to break," Julie said.

All of them left the street and headed back to their vehicles and drove away. The Sheriff called one of his deputies into his office, "Follow them and see what they're up to and let me know if they do anything not normal."

"Yes sir," The deputy said, as he left the office not sure what not normal was.

The Sheriff watched the two vehicles drive away down the street and laughed to himself, "Giant cannibals, what the heck are they drinking and smoking over in Utah?"

After getting their rooms at the motel, they decided it was time to go get something to eat. That's when Jim told the others that he noticed that they were being followed by someone in uniform. They all went into the restaurant, and sitting down, looked out the window, saw the man sitting across the street in his car.

"Just as I thought, not only do they think were crazy, but now they're following us to make sure we don't do anything stupid," Jim said.

"What did you expect from these non-believers Jim? They must think we're all nuts from Utah, with the story we told him." the Dean replied.

"If I didn't know any better I would have a hard time believing what we just told the Sheriff, myself," said Professor Wainwright.

"It does seem farfetched, doesn't it," Jim replied.

"Let's order some food, I'm really hungry right now," Julie said.

They looked at their menus and ordered dinner. In an hour they were done and got up to leave. Getting back to their motel rooms, Jim lay down on the bed and pretended to be asleep. Julie lay down next to him being just as tired and was out in seconds. Jim nudged her and whispered in her ear to make sure she was asleep, after checking to make sure, he got up and watched the news on the local channel. He knew that the Dean and the Professor were in their room fast asleep. Finding nothing of interest on the local news channel, Jim turned off the TV and lay back down next to Julie and went to sleep, as well. Whatever happens tonight would have to wait till tomorrow morning to be dealt with by the crazy professors from Utah.

The deputy decided that with them asleep in their rooms he would knock off for the night, as well, and go home to get some sleep and take another crack at it tomorrow morning after breakfast. Driving back to the Sheriff's office, he reported in to dispatch, "I'm off for the night, see you in the morning."

Chapter VII

In two hours, the creature was fully recovered from his wounds after fighting the grizzly bear and once again he was hungry for food. Stepping out of the trees he had been laying in, he started looking around for something to eat. This time, smelling the air, he caught the scent of man again and following his nose he ran down the side of the mountain looking for his next meal. As it just so happened, there was another family camping near the river, the old man was fishing, and the kids were playing near the camp. The mom was reading a book in her chair watching the kids play in between reading pages of her book. The dog was barking with the kids as he played with them.

The creature, looking around, made sure there would be no surprises when he went in for the kill. As he got closer, the dog heard him and then smelled him, looking in the direction of the trees. The mom saw how the dog was acting and got up to look around the camp site. Now the hair on the back of the dog was standing straight up and he was growling. Not seeing anything for the moment, the mom started to get the feeling that something was watching them. Calling the kids and then to her husband, he came out of the river, "What's wrong dear."

"Look at Buck and how he is acting," she said.

Seeing the dog growling and that the hair on his back was up, and looking into the forest, the kids were starting to be afraid and got closer to their parents. The father put down his fishing pole and went in and grabbed his gun and waited to see what it was that the dog had alerted on. All of them standing there were now watching the woods, not sure of what to be looking for or what they were looking at.

The creature realizing his chance to catch one of them off guard was gone now, gave up and moved on to find easier prey. A few minutes after leaving the family alone, finally the dog relaxed as he continued to watch the woods for a while. Eventually, everything went back to normal and the kids started playing again. This time the mom turned her chair facing the woods and the children, keeping an eye on them all, as she pretended to read her book.

The creature started making his way down into the valley where the city was located. Passing farmland, he saw sheep in the pasture and decided that would be his next meal.

Waiting till dark, the creature again found a clump of trees to hide in and watched the sheep until he was ready to make his move. Moving down the mountain when it was dark, he grabbed a couple of sheep. He carried them off to the end of the pasture and ate them, leaving only the blood and what was left of the carcasses in the field. The creature then moved back to the clump of trees to rest. It wouldn't be until the next day that the sheep would be found mutilated, by the sheep herder. He would report it to the Sheriff's department, and by then the local reporter, listening to a police scanner, would check it to see if it was news worthy and if so would run it on the air for the local news.

Jim was taking a shower when the news on the radio reported that two sheep had been found in the pasture mutilated. Julie caught the story as she was putting on her makeup after her shower. Walking into the bathroom, she told Jim what she had just heard on the news report from the radio. Jim said, "Call your dad to let them know that we might have something to go check out in the pasture."

Jim quickly finished his shower and was dressed in a few minutes after drying off, just in time for Julie to be finished, as well. Meeting the Dean and the Professor, who were already outside waiting by their vehicle and watching a family as they brought groceries out of their truck into their motel room. They couldn't help but notice a big hole in the side of his pickup bed. Not wanting to waste any of their time and being excited about the possibility of the Dean's plan actually working, they all got in one of their vehicles and drove down to the radio station to talk to the people there. When they arrived at the radio station, Jim got out and went into the building while the others sat in the jeep and waited.

Jim asked the secretary, "You guys ran a report earlier today about some sheep being mutilated?"

The secretary shook her head, yes, "It happened last night at the end of one of the pastures where the sheep were grazing,"

"Can you tell us where to find this place?"

Again, she nodded yes, "Go to the end of main street and turn left on the main road, go about two miles outside of town on Miller Road and follow it until you get to the fork in the road, then go left and the pasture should be on the left as well. At the end of that you will find what's left of the sheep."

Jim was writing all of this down on a piece of paper as she gave him the directions, when complete he thanked her for the information. As he was walking out the secretary said, "I don't know if you heard or not but a couple of days ago a man and his family were attacked by something that he claims was a giant, at night at their place just outside of town as he got back from a trip to Denver. Jim stopped in his tracks and turned around, "Where can I find this man and his family?"

"He is staying at the local motel in town. He claims it destroyed his house, killed his dog, and scared his wife so bad she won't go back to their place anymore. Not that there is anything to go back to. From what I understand, the giant destroyed the house completely."

"Is there anything else you can tell me about this giant?"

"Rumor has it, that two deputies were hurt when they went to check it out."

Jim thanked her again then said to himself as he walked away, "Geez, no wonder the Sheriff seemed edgy when we told him what we knew about it."

Jim got back into the Jeep and headed back to the motel to talk to the family that they had seen earlier. As he drove back, Jim explained why they were headed back to the motel. All of them agreed with Jim and were anxious to meet the family. Knocking on the motel room door where the family was staying, the father answered the door and seeing all four of them standing there asked, "You guys from the government?"

Surprised by the question, they all stood there for a moment not knowing what to say. Finally, Professor Wainwright spoke up, "Are you the gentleman who was attacked by something in the night and in the process lost your home?"

"Look, if you're here to make fun of me about this, you are already too late everybody in town has beat you to it."

"Please forgive my friends and I, we mean you no disrespect. We actually believe you and your story about what happened that night," the Dean said.

"What would you like to know about it?"

"First of all, can we come in and talk to you about your experience? Please forgive me, my manners are somewhat lacking, my name is Professor Wainwright, and we are from Brigham Young University. This is Jim, and my daughter, Julie, and this old grizzled man, is the Dean at our school we are all archeologists. We're very much interested in finding out what happened that night when this took place."

"I came in on the tail end of it myself, however, my wife was there from the beginning of it. You should ask her about it," said the father.

With all of them looking at his wife, waiting for her to start, she sat down first and then started, "We had just finished dinner and I was cleaning up the table, when our dog, Sammy, started barking and wanting to go outside. Opening the patio door, I let him out, he continued barking. I figured it was deer in the yard, so I sent Johnny our son to go get the dog and bring him back in or at least to get him to stop barking. It was at this point, I heard Sammy yelp, and then the barking stopped. I looked outside and didn't see Johnny anywhere, so I went out to go look for him. I called for him, but there was no answer. I started looking in the back yard and that's when I saw Sammy laying in the yard half eaten. I didn't know what to do, I have to tell you, I was really scared by now."

As she sat there in her chair everybody could see that she was having a hard time dealing with what had happened. Jim and Julie were writing everything down on paper as she spoke. By now, the lady was crying and her husband came and put his arm around her to help her regain her composure. Julie handed her some tissues to wipe her eyes as she continued with her story, "I looked for Johnny and couldn't find him anywhere in the yard. And then I heard this blood curdling scream and I just about lost it. I ran back into the house, turning on all of the lights in the house, hoping the lights would scare away whatever it was out there. I grabbed my daughter and we sat on the swing in our porch, not doing or saying anything. We stayed there until my husband showed up. I gotta tell you, I've heard mountain lions scream but this was totally different. I've never heard anything like it before. As we sat in the shadows, I think I saw something that walked on two feet and stood about twelve feet tall. From what I could tell his face was human, but his mouth was really strange looking."

The Dean left the room for a minute, going back to his room and came back with a file with some pictures in it. Laying the pictures out on the small table in their room, he handed her one of the pictures, "Did it look like this?"

The woman studied the picture and the tears came on again as she nodded her head, yes. She looked up at the Dean, "What is it?"

The Dean looked at the others as she passed the picture to her husband and he studied the picture and the others on the table, as well. Both of the parents were looking at the Dean, waiting to hear what he had to say, "Well for one thing, we believe you saw something that has been dead for over three thousand years and to be honest with you, you're all lucky to be alive after running into this creature."

"That's what the Sheriff said when we went back the next day to look at the mess that we once called a house," the father said.

Jim went ahead and started to tell them what it was and how they had been destroyed a long time ago by others like him, but more peaceful than this one. When he was done explaining things to them, the father said, "You really believe us on this, we're not going crazy?"

"Not by a long shot, we're here to take it back to where it came from and put it back in its place where it will never bother anyone ever again," Jim said.

"If what you say is true, how do you plan on doing that?"

"To be honest with you, you wouldn't believe me if I told you," and clearing his throat he continued, "We're going to be the bait to draw him back to where he came from."

"You're right, I don't believe you, but that being said, I wish you luck," the father said, as he looked at them kind of crazy.

The whole family now started looking at all the pictures that the Dean had brought over, realizing that they had truly had been blessed to be alive. The wife just sat there, holding onto her son, Johnny, telling her husband how much she loved him for going back to find their son. The husband looked relieved that there were people who finally believed him and his wife, about what they seen that night.

"The only problem is that the creature is still around here. We believe he killed some farmers sheep not too far from here. We were on our way to look at the remains of the sheep when the secretary at the radio station told us about your experience from the other night," Jim said.

"And if that's the case, the sheep were killed by this creature. You don't want to be out at night right now, in other words stay inside till we tell you different," Julie said.

"Not to worry about that, we don't leave the room unless It's light outside," the father said.

"Probably a good idea, and oh, one more thing, please keep this to yourselves, if you will. I'm afraid there may be a panic if this was to get out right now. We need time to get him back without the local people going nuts," Professor Wainwright said.

"I don't think that's going to be a problem, nobody around here believes us anyway," the mother said.

With that, all four of them left to go look at the dead sheep in the pasture. As the Dean gathered his pictures to take with him, the mother and father shook their hands as they left the room, "Thank you for believing our story and restoring our sanity and peace of mind."

"In some ways, your family is lucky to have seen something that has been dead for over three thousand years. That being said, I'm sorry you and your family had to deal with this creature in this way. I wish you all the luck in the world from this point on."

Jim sat in the jeep waiting for the others to get in and as he sat there he said aloud, "I'm thinking I now understand why Red Hawk doesn't want this to get out to the public just yet, think of the panic it could cause if it did get out."

"I guarantee you that if those people hadn't seen it with their own eyes, they would think we were nuts, as well," Julie replied.

"Tell you the truth, I think we are nuts for what we are trying to do," the Professor said.

The deputy called the Sheriff, letting him know that the team from Utah had been by to visit the family that lost their home and dog. Upon hearing this, he told the deputy, "Keep me posted on anything else going on with these guys."

"Will do."

The Sheriff wondered why they would be visiting there at the motel with the family. May be there is something to what they were telling him.

As the four of them stood there looking at the remains of the sheep, it was obvious that whatever had done this was brutal in their attack. The pieces of the sheep were all over the place, as if there was no rhyme or reason to any of it. At this point, Julie said, "I wonder if the same thing is going to happen to us, if we go after this creature?"

All of them were thinking the same thing and no one really knew how to answer the question Julie had posed to them. Getting back into the Jeep, they were quiet all the way back to their motel rooms. Each of them were lost in their own thoughts about what they were trying to do. Opening the door to their room, Julie started crying as she entered the room from being scared. Jim, closing the door behind him, came over and put his arms around her and tried to calm her down. He understood perfectly what she was feeling because he felt the same way as she did. Sitting on their bed, offering a prayer to help them, and strengthen them in this endeavor, was all they could think of doing at the moment. The Dean and the Professor were feeling overwhelmed with the task that lay before them, as well, and offering a prayer, they pleaded for guidance and strength. They all knew the creature would be striking again and hopefully it would be sheep or cattle again for his next meal, and not humans.

The deputy sat in his car and watched the motel for the rest of the evening. As it was, each of them ordered out for dinner to be delivered to their rooms. The deputy went home about ten o'clock himself, tired from doing nothing but sitting in the squad car all day.

Staying close to Julie, Jim made sure that the door to their room was locked and bolted for his piece of mind. Julie lay awake for a while after Jim fell asleep, wondering how things were going to turn out, thinking about what happened the last time they were in Colorado.

The creature had been filled up on sheep meat and would sleep the night away, up on the mountain in a clump of trees, overlooking the pasture where he had found a good source for food. Therefore, tonight the town would be safe, for the time being.

Chapter VIII

The next morning came as usual and the local radio news hadn't reported anything out of the ordinary from the previous night. Jim and Julie were still in bed and lightly sleeping when the phone rang in their room. Jim picked it up, answering it still half asleep. It was the Professor on the other end of the phone apologizing for calling so early.

"What's up?" Jim asked.

"I was just thinking that we need to move the creature back into the mountains, right?"

"Right," he said half listening.

"I think I may have come up with an idea on how to do that. I'm thinking if we use bait like they do to attract sharks when they chum the waters, it might work the same way, drawing him back to the valley."

Jim, wide awake now, was thinking about what the Professor said.

"Are you still there Jim?" the Professor asked.

"Yes, yes, I am, and I think you may be right in your thinking Professor," Jim said, now fully awake.

"The problem is, we need some drivers to push the creature back in the direction we want him to go. I don't know of anybody that would be willing to do that, do you?"

"How about the Sheriff and his deputies doing it for us?"

"How do we convince the Sheriff that the creature is real?"

"You know the one deputy that is following us, don't you? Have him follow us and then invite him to go with us."

"How are we to get the creature to come to us to prove our point?"

"Chumming in a sense. We set a trap to catch him with bait, so that the deputy can report back to the Sheriff that what we told him was real about the creature. Then maybe we can get his help."

"So, when do you want to do this?"

"How about tonight. We know the creature has found a food source and will not go anywhere else until he runs out of the food first. Let's set the trap with some fresh meat and then wait and see. Hopefully, we can get pictures of him eating, then we will have our proof for the Sheriff."

"Kind of like the hunting the way they do in Texas, where they have a feeder setup to draw the animals in at a certain time. Then the hunters can pick and choose the animals that they want to shoot."

"You got it, and if everything goes right the Sheriff, seeing the creature, will be thanking us when we take him out of the valley."

"When do we start?"

"That's the reason I'm calling so early. If we can get going on it now, then most likely we should be set by this evening."

Jim was sitting up in bed by now and Julie was just starting to wake up, somewhat listening to the conversation. Jim reached over and touched her on the arm, "Your dad has an idea about catching the creature on camera tonight, so we can convince the Sheriff to help us."

Julie was now starting to wake up when she heard Jim say, "Give us an hour and we should be ready to go, after breakfast to set this up."

"Not a problem Jim, I still need to run this by the Dean myself when he wakes up."

As promised, in an hour Jim and Julie were ready to go and met the Dean and the Professor outside the hotel, stopping to eat breakfast first. They finished eating then headed out to get the meat, the camera equipment, the lighting system, and other miscellaneous stuff, in order to attract the creature towards them.

By now, the deputy now back on the job, was following them and getting curious about what they were doing and why they were going to the hardware store. Deciding to call the Sheriff, he let him know that the people from Utah were busy going all over town getting supplies and stuff together. The biggest question that came up was, why they would be going to the hardware store to get lights, motion operated cameras, and fence posts. The deputy started taking pictures with his cell phone while the team went on about their business of collecting the things they needed.

Their next stop was to contact the farmer, who had lost the sheep, and talk to him to get his permission to set up the equipment on his land in the pasture to catch the creature in the act of trying to kill more of his sheep. At first, the farmer thought they were nuts, but after some convincing the farmer agreed, more out of curiosity than anything else, to let them do it. The farmer was really interested in catching the animal that was killing his sheep and the team told him it was probably a grizzly bear, that had come out of the mountains, hungry for some easy food.

Having everything they needed on hand plus the permission from the farmer to use his land, the team went about setting the stage to catch the creature in the act of eating the meat in order to convince the Sheriff to help them. The deputy, who had been watching all of this, now pretty much knew what was going on, and reported this to the Sheriff, who was now interested in it, as well. Later in the day the Sheriff came by as they were setting up the cameras on the poles, and looking around said, "So you think you're going to photograph this creature in the process of eating the sheep?"

"How else can we convince you that this creature is real? In fact, why don't you come out here tonight and join us on our hunting expedition and see for yourself," Jim said, looking at the Sheriff.

"I might just do that, about what time are we talking about?"

"About nine o'clock, maybe ten."

"Which one of you is going to be the bait?" the Sheriff asked, smiling.

"If you get here soon enough, it could be you Sheriff," Jim said, without missing a beat.

The smile on the Sheriff's face went away quickly after Jim's remark and as he walked away, Jim could hear him cussing under his breath. Jim smiled, and Julie asked as she walked over, "What was that all about?"

"Just trying to invite the Sheriff out tonight to see the show."

"Did it work, did he say yes?"

"I'm not sure, he said he would have to think about it some more."

In an hour, the stage was set and ready to go, now all they needed was to get the meat out of the cooler. They decided to wait to get the meat out until later in the evening when they got themselves set up in the tent. At this point they also needed to buy a hunting blind for them to sit inside, while waiting for the creature to strike, plus a couple of shotguns to protect themselves, just in case things got out of hand. The shotguns didn't need a time delay in order to buy them and could be picked up on the same day they purchased them. They also picked up some heavy duty shot shells for self-defense that would fit the bill, in case it was necessary to shoot the creature. Jim and the Professor would be sitting inside the blind, waiting for the creature to make his appearance tonight. They both knew they couldn't kill the creature, but they could hurt it just enough to make it think twice about not wanting to come after them again.

Once all of this was complete it was just a matter of waiting for the creature to appear, and hopefully, that would be tonight. By now, it was dinner time, and having everything completed they all headed to the local café to eat before going back to the pasture later in the evening. Stopping by where the deputy was parked while watching them before heading out, they invited him to go along with them to eat. At first surprised, he thought about it for a minute, "Why not, it's better than sitting this car watching you eat."

When they got to the café they all sat down, the waitress came over to their table, "Are you the guys trying to catch some kind of creature on the cameras out in old man Joe's sheep pasture?"

Realizing that the gossip was faster than what they had thought, the Dean, looking up from the menu said, "What we're looking for is a creature that is three thousand years old and get him on camera to show that the creature does exist. It's considered to be a cannibal and eats human beings whenever it can, and worse than that, he can't be killed except with a silver bullet and a burning cross with a wooden stake driven into its heart."

All of them were smiling as they continued looking at their menus, including the deputy. It took a second for the waitress to realize that the Dean was pulling her leg and she laughed at what the Dean had said, "You're pulling my leg aren't you?"

"Are you sure I am, little lady?" the Dean said, with a serious look on his face.

By now, the waitress couldn't tell whether the Dean was pulling her leg or not. Not sure what to do she said, "You guys let me know when you are ready to order, in the meantime I'll get all your drinks."

Each of them watched the waitress go back and get their waters to drink and as she did so she stood there talking to one of the other waitresses and pointing her finger at them. The deputy smiled, "Telephone, telegraph, or tell Betty the waitress either way it'll get out through the news service."

They all laughed at the comment by the deputy and waited for their water to show up. After taking their orders that the waitress brought their food but didn't stay long around them. The rest of the evening was spent talking and discussing their plans on catching the creature in the act. The deputy just sat there listening to their talk, trying to decide if what they were saying would work. When they were all finished with dinner they headed back out to the field.

By now, it was getting dark and the creature was feeling hungry again and knowing where the food source was, just waited for the right time to make his move. The Professor and Jim were throwing out meat onto the ground to attract the creature to come down to them, starting at the fence post and moving deeper into the pasture to where the hunting blind was located. By nine o'clock, having gotten into the hunting blind, all was ready for the creature and everybody was in their places, waiting for the creature to show. As the creature made its way down the mountain, he caught the smell of fresh meat that was different from the sheep he had smelled the day before. This was more to his liking and now he hurried to find it. Coming closer to the pasture the creature saw the tent further back in the field and posts in the ground. The creature stopped, waiting to see if there was any movement from any of the new stuff in the field. Realizing there were none, and being hungry, he overrode the issue of the safety threat to him. He then moved down the mountain and into the field to find the source of the smell. Jim and the Professor were inside the blind sitting and waiting for the creature to show, they were caught off guard by how quiet the creature was when they heard the Dean say over the radio,

"I'm picking up some movement at the fence line coming towards you guys."

"Roger that," Jim replied, as he pushed the safety off of the shotgun he was holding and pointed it down range through the opening of the blind.

All of the team, including the deputy, now held their breath as the creature came down to check out the new smell of the meat. Getting closer and moving past the posts in the field, the cameras started flashing as they took pictures as he passed by the cameras. The creature stopped and waited to see what would happen with the flashing cameras. Seeing no reaction from the cameras, the creature kept pressing forward towards the meat that had been stacked up in the center of the field. The creature, looked around, and seeing no one there, proceeded to start eating the meat. The deputy, with his binoculars, watched the creature as he squatted and began to eat. At this point, all he could say was, "Holy crap, look at the size of that damn thing, and his face, what's with his face?"

Julie grabbed the Dean's binder full of pictures, and finding the right one said, "Does it look like this?"

The deputy studied the picture, "Yes, and uglier."

"His mouth has two sets of teeth made for tearing meat from off the bones of animals and humans. Count, if you can, how many fingers he has on his hands. There should be six on each hand," the Dean said.

"I believe you," the deputy said, as he continued to watch the creature through the field glasses.

The Dean continued to watch through his own field glasses, as well, while Jim and the Professor started taking pictures of the creature from inside the blind. Jim held the shotgun while the Professor did the honors of the picture taking. When the creature was done eating he stood up, and looking around, screamed out his call and turned around, walking back up into the mountain, disappearing into the darkness once again. The deputy put down his glasses and looked at the Dean, "You know you weren't too far off from what you told the waitress back at the café."

The Dean smiled, "Yeah I know, but the burning stake and silver bullet won't kill that thing that you just saw."

"So how do you kill it?"

"We don't, we just return it back to where it came from and let the other people do their thing."

"I don't understand."

"Believe me when I say, I'm not sure I do either."

By now, the two of them left their spot further back in the field and started walking down to where the blind was. They watched Jim gather the S memory cards out of the motion cameras on the poles, so he could download the pictures from them, to show the Sheriff. With the deputy seeing it as well, it would be hard disproving what the team had been saying all along. Unbeknownst to everybody the Sheriff had seen everything from his vantage point and just stood there not knowing whether to trust his eyes or pinch himself too check to see if he was awake or in a real live nightmare.

The family at the motel heard the cry from the creature, and as they sat in their room looking at each other, the wife was starting to react all over again from the flashback of being at their house once more. She ran around the motel room, making sure her kids were all there with her and sleeping peacefully, before settling down again. Laying down next to her husband on the bed, shaking with fear. All her husband could do was hold and comfort her, to keep her from shaking anymore. Even with him holding her she couldn't hold back the tears of fear.

The next day the team went back to the Sheriff's office to talk to him, and this time he was waiting for them to show up. He was almost human to them, especially, after seeing the pictures taken by the Professor from the night before from inside the blind. In fact, Jim was surprised by how agreeable he was, "How come such a change from the last time we talked, Sheriff?"

"I was out there last night as well, watching what you guys were doing and I saw the creature. We're lucky nobody has died yet from this thing, including my two deputies."

"Yes, you are Sheriff," Jim said

"Is there any way to capture it?"

"I don't know, but if you have any ideas we'd be open to them," Professor Wainwright said.

The Sheriff started thinking about people he knew that might be able to assist in this, and sitting down again at his desk, started flipping through his rolodex looking for names.

"We were thinking that we could lead him back to where he came from by leading the creature with meat. Kind of like we did to get his pictures taken last night. The problem is, we would need to have some men as drivers to force him back into the mountains where he came from, once again," Jim said.

"I take it, you want us to drive him back into the woods for you, while you lead him with food to keep him going in the right direction," the Sheriff said.

"We aren't even sure that this will be guaranteed to work. But that's all that we could come up with," the Professor said.

"Have you given any thought about capturing him and putting him in a cage and taking him back to where he belongs?" the Sheriff asked.

As the group considered the Sheriff's idea, Jim said, "I like your idea of catching him and putting him inside a cage, I just don't know if there is anything big enough to carry him in, without the creature being able to break out of it."

"We could use a grizzly bear cage, that should be strong enough to hold him," the Sheriff replied.

"The real question is, how do we get him into it without getting anybody killed in the process?" Julie asked.

"We could tranquilize him with a sedative and keep him sedated till we get him into the cage, from there we can transport the creature to where he needs to go," Jim replied.

"I know that the forest service has the equipment and the drugs for putting down bears to relocate them away from the humans," the Sheriff said.

"That's good, now how do we go about borrowing it, without telling them why?" the Dean asked.

"We could tell them were doing a drug bust and need the cage to hold the extra drugs we might come across in the raid."

"Do you think that will work Sheriff?"

"I don't know, it's never been tried before."

"Whatever we do, we need to find the creature first and then bring him into the cage to hold him. Sheriff, do you know anybody that can track the creature, that won't talk about it later for publicity purposes?" Jim asked.

"I think I do and he won't talk about it to anyone, I'll give him a call. I just wonder if he'll talk to me after I got his best dogs killed the first time while tracking the creature."

"We have to try, maybe if we show him the pictures that might help in his decision."

"Okay, I'll do it then. But just don't be too surprised if he turns us down."

"I think if he sees the pictures he'll help us, if for nothing else, then to get even for what the creature did to his dogs."

Chapter IX

The Sheriff called Bill Mortenson at his house, wondering what kind of reception he would get from him once he knew who he was talking to. His last talk with him hadn't gone very well and he was wondering if Bill would hang up on him before he was able to speak to him, praying that he wouldn't hang up before telling him he was needed again.

Bill picked up the phone on the fourth ring, "Hello."

The Sheriff identified himself, "Bill it's the Sheriff, can you come down to the station right now, we need you to do something for us."

"I thought that I wasn't man enough for what you needed done."

"I apologize for my remark Bill, I was wrong when I said it."

Thinking for a moment, "I'll be right down then."

As he got his coat and walked out of his house to his truck, he said to himself, "I wonder what's going on that the Sheriff, who never apologizes to anyone, now needs me?"

When Bill got down to the station he was sent directly into Sheriff's office by the secretary. As he walked into the Sheriff's office he saw that it was crowded with others he hadn't met before. As the Sheriff introduced the team from Utah to him he was surprised to see them there.

As everybody sat down in their chairs once more, the Sheriff, looking at Bill, handed him the pictures taken from the night before. Bill took a minute in order to digest them for his benefit. He studied them for a while before the Sheriff went on to say, "This is what your dog's ran into on the mountain, that's what got them killed and also tried to kill two of my deputies."

Bill, setting the pictures down, shook his head, "What is it, I've never seen anything like this before."

"We call it the creature. This one is about three thousand years old. He is considered a cannibal, it has six fingers and six toes and a double set of teeth in its mouth and you can't kill it," Jim said, as he looked at Bill.

"So why am I here then, this damn thing killed my best dogs and you're telling me you can't kill it?"

"Even if you shoot it and hit it with a shotgun or anything else, it will eventually heal itself back to normal. We need you to track it down for us, so that we can shoot it with a tranquilizer, capture it, and then take it back in a cage to where it came from," the Professor said.

Bill thought about what had been said, and looking at the Sheriff and the others said, "When do we start?"

"As soon as we can find a cage big enough and strong enough to hold it. You are our best tracker in the county and you will take the lead and we'll follow you."

"Hopefully, not too far behind me. I don't want to run into that thing on my own."

"I'll be with you with a shotgun and also an AR-15 with me as well," the Sheriff replied.

"Yeah that's good for you, but what about me? What do I get to carry to give me a false sense of security?"

"How about another shotgun with double odd buckshot in it?"

"Works for me."

As the team of Sheriff's deputies and the Utah professors proceeded to lay out their plans on how to capture the creature, they were busy trying to find a location to hold the creature to get it to where the cage could be used to hold him. All of them were concerned about the creature coming to and regaining his strength before getting him into the cage and maybe killing someone in the process. The creature was considered pretty strong just due to its size. The sedative to be used would have to be strong enough to stop an elephant in its tracks and had to last long enough to get him in the cage.

The plan was to drive the creature by noise and or force, if necessary, to a known location where the cage would be close enough to put him in. And have enough men to drag or carry him to the cage. That was the plan now, whether it worked or not was the sixty-four-thousand-dollar question.

The secretary came into the Sheriff's office to let him know that the BLM (Bureau of Land Management) personnel had called back saying, that the use of the bear cage was good to go and available and ready for pick up. The Sheriff dispatched two of his deputies to go get it from them and bring it back to the staging area on the mountain.

Finally, with all of the plans were worked out, the question now became when were they were going to do this. The Sheriff didn't want a panic on his hands when it came to the creature, yet at the same time he needed enough men to do the job of the drivers. The Dean said that he would be one of the drivers while Jim and Professor Wainwright would be the ones with the dart gun with the sedative, waiting to take the shot. Julie would stay with the Sheriff to coordinate the drivers. Bill would lead the drivers as he tracked the creature to begin the drive. He would be the one in danger most of the time as he looked for and tracked the creature. Along with the Sheriff and Julie, he would also have two other men with him with shotguns as well.

They decided to do the drive during the daylight hours that way there would be less chance of having the creature slip by them, it would be safer this way, as well, for all involved. They all agreed that they would begin tomorrow morning at sunrise. Bill was shown where the creature came down the mountain to eat and that would be the starting point. Having two other dogs that were not as good as his others, was all he could offer at this point and they would have to do. The rest of the day was spent putting the cage together and placing it close to where the command center would be.

Now it was time to look for volunteers to be the drivers. Calling in all of his deputies, the Sheriff explained what was going on and showed them the pictures of the creature, to let them know what they were up against. All of the deputies agreed to help and that, for this operation, would be enough people needed to have as drivers. Once everything was accomplished, each of the players in this operation prepared themselves by checking their weapons and gear to be ready. Jim and the Professor were able to go over to the vet's office to get the dart gun and tranquilizer, and to get trained in its use. The vet would be part of the team in the command center to monitor the creature for anything out of the unusual and if anything went south in the process. The vet knew very well that this was a highly unusual situation and his best educated guess for stopping the creature, would have to work for all concerned or people could die.

As Jim, and the others from Utah, sat at the table eating their dinners, each was running through their heads the part they would play in tomorrow's adventure, escapade, fool's mission, suicide mission, you name it. Each of them saw it their own way, but the real thought on everybody's mind was, would it work without anybody getting hurt. Only time would tell, and they would only know that by tomorrow night, and only if they were able to catch the creature.

Later that evening, Jim and Julie were inside their room watching the late news on TV. Each of them, not able to sleep, or for that matter being tired. They just lay on the bed, stressed and thinking about the upcoming events for the next day. Jim got up and walked to the small refrigerator to get something to drink. Having picked up a six pack of coke, he decided to have one. Sitting in one of the chairs in the room he looked out the window and wondered what tomorrow would bring, good news or bad news. He wondered how they got into this situation and if there would be any more like it in the future for both of them.

Julie, feeling Jim was gone from her side, sat up in bed and saw him looking out the window, "Is everything alright Jim?"

"Yes, I'm alright and no, I'm worried about tomorrow and how it will turn out for us."

"Yeah, me too. I can't help but think about the family who lost their house and almost their lives, and how it will never be the same for them ever again."

"I still can't get over the size of the creature and how he's trapped in our world. A misfit in his time and a bigger misfit in our time."

"What happens tomorrow if we can't catch the beast?"

"That's the easy part, we keep going until we do capture him and take him back to the valley."

As he came back to bed, he reached over to Julie and held her, "We'll get through this and all will be well in the end."

"I hope you're right, in fact, I'm praying you're right."

In the other motel room, the Dean and the Professor were awake as well, thinking about tomorrow and going through all of the options they had, as far as catching the creature. In some ways, it was a hunt for something neither of them knew existed until that time in the valley two years ago. The Professor was worried about his daughter Julie, simply because she had been looking weak and pale this whole time he had been with her on this trip and not knowing why. He had asked her about it, but her answer was the same each time, she was just tired from all of what was going on. He realized the excitement of dealing with the creature and setting up the traps, cameras, and such had taken their toll on her. The Professor said a silent prayer for his daughter, hoping she would be okay. Jim had been doing the same thing for her, but didn't let her know about it.

Julie had gotten more tired recently and couldn't understand why. She slept more, ate less in the morning, and made up for it in the afternoon. She didn't understand any of this and wasn't sure what to do about it, except just go with it, leastwise, until they got back to Provo and set up an appointment with her regular doctor. When that would be was up in the air, seeing as how, they were about to go hunting for a creature that wasn't supposed to exist. By the time the news was over for the night, all of them went to sleep, hoping and praying for some good news come tomorrow evening.

The Sheriff, watching out of his office window, wondered what kind of creature this was and where did it come from originally, three thousand years ago. All of his patrols being carried out for the county were now being carried out by two deputies per car. No one would ride alone until this creature was caught and taken away. The town of Castlerock was very much aware that something was going on since the pictures had been taken of the creature. Whether the people believed or not didn't matter, nobody was willing to take the chance that it could be real. For the first time, no one was on the streets after dark which made it easier for the deputies to do their jobs at night.

The story of the house, a squad car being torn up, and two deputies being hurt dealing with some sort of giant had reached the ears of the Director in Colorado Springs. The rumor that it was a giant man creature who had done all of this, was very interesting to the Director. Dispatching a couple of his agents to go check it out, he hoped it was what he thought it was. If it was all true, this would make a big difference in his line of work. If it was true it would be a major advancement in his research and development of the perfect soldier. Having a live creature would be the opportunity of a life time to be able to experiment on.

Chapter X

The next morning, they all awoke and as they looked out the window they could tell it had rained during the night, there was a low cloud bank over the valley. By breakfast time the cloud had started to dissipate and burn off from the morning sun. The trail would be easy to follow, even with the rainfall from the night before. With the rain, the air was fresh and clean, and felt good as they stood there together, waiting for the Sheriff to come out of his office building and have everybody load up in their trucks to go to the command post in the field.

The creature, who had found some trees to take cover in, was just waking up himself, completely wet and as usual, he was hungry and was restless to get some food to eat. Clean air from the rain the night before aided in being able to smell animals in the forest. A grizzly bear, who was in the area also, was hungry as well. Looking for something to eat, he stood on his hind legs and could smell the creature once more. Remembering the last time they had encountered each other, he went the other way to avoid the creature. The creature was walking through the forest, stopping every so often to smell the air. Finding no scents to follow, he was getting angry for not being able to find any food to eat. He let out a howl out of frustration and the Sheriff and the others heard its cry. The Sheriff looked at everyone gathered together and smiled, "At least we know he's still here."

Everybody that was there, kind of nervously laughed a little and went about making sure they were ready for each of their parts. The teams loaded up into their trucks and drove to Joe's pasture. From there they unloaded all of the parts for the cage and started getting it ready to carry from there to another spot on the other side of the mountain. It would take two hours of hiking up the mountain to get to the place where they would set it up. Each piece of the cage took two men to carry and upon arriving on the other side of the mountain they started working to put it together. They had armed guards to watch over everyone that was there to set up the cage. Each man knew what would happen if they failed to do their part in this endeavor, somebody could get hurt or even die and nobody wanted to be the reason for that. Another incentive was that each of them didn't want to be the reason for this operation to fail.

As the men put the cage together, Jim and the Professor, still in their truck, continued on down the road. Each of the teams had radios to coordinate all of their movements in locating the creature.

Jim and the Professor would take the far point and, hopefully, place the creature between them and the drivers, and just wait for the drivers to bring the creature to them. Finding a place a couple of miles in front of the group of drivers, they set up their spot in the trees. Climbing the bigger trees, they made themselves comfortable sitting in some portable tree stands, being mixed within the branches of the trees. Granted, their smell would be found out by the creature before even being seen. Hopefully, it would give them the extra time they would need to shoot the creature with the tranquillizer gun before getting hurt. Once they were set up in their spot, Jim called on the radio, "We're ready to go whenever you are."

The Sheriff, receiving the message from Jim and the Professor, looked at Bill and gave the signal to start following the tracks of the beast. The other deputies were fanned out on the left and right side of the Sheriff, in sight of each other and started to bang pots and pans to distract the creature. Walking behind Bill and the Sheriff by a couple of paces, the drivers started making their way up the mountain. Bill, with his two dogs on short leashes, started moving forward, being pulled by the dogs as they searched for the scent of the creature.

The creature could hear the banging noise coming from the deputies as they made their way up the mountain and not sure to what make of it he went back in the direction of the noise to check it out. From his rocky perch he could see that the noise was coming from a line of men that were slowly advancing towards him. He could also hear the barking of dogs and at this point he wasn't sure what to do. Remembering what had happened the last time he had an encounter with humans and dogs he let out a howl as he decided to keep moving deeper into the woods to get away from the threat. The issue of being hungry was now replaced with survival and getting away from the men down below who were making the noise. Running and then stopping to see where the men were, he would take off again in a different direction. The line of men was long and the creature realized that all he could do was to keep running in the opposite direction of the noise.

The drivers weren't sure if what they were doing was working or not, all they could do was keep moving forward, hoping it was doing the trick. At one point, the creature was forced out into the open and was seen by a couple of the drivers. Howling at the two men, the creature made his way onto a small rise and waited to attack them from his hiding place in the trees. The creature now was mad and, on the offensive, waiting for the drivers to show, so he could eliminate the threat. The drivers knew he was in the area and proceeded with caution. Sensing that the creature was near, one of the drivers pulled his shotgun into firing position and walked slowly with the other drivers in the lead. Just as they got close to where the creature was, he attacked the line. Going after the two closest men, he hit them full force, one of the drivers went down while the other fired his shotgun at the creature. The other drivers pulled out their shotguns and started firing at the creature, moving fast he was able to avoid most of the blasts and was able to stay out of the line of fire. But a few of the shooters, seeing this, compensated for this and started aiming in front of the creature, leading him and hitting him with buckshot. Being hit with the double odd buckshot in the legs, it slowed the creature down. Realizing that he couldn't out run the men because of his wounds made him more furious. He then turned around and attacked the men again, this time taking two of the drivers out by hitting them with his fists and knocking them senseless, dropping them to the ground.

The other drivers, seeing this, closed ranks on the creature and continued firing at him, hitting him numerous times now. This time the shots hit their mark and he started howling in pain from being hit. The two men that had been attacked were pulled from the area by some others, while the other deputies continued firing at the creature, providing cover for those retrieving the injured. Firing point blank at the creature and hitting him in the main torso, the creature pulled back away from the drivers bleeding from the wounds inflicted by the shotguns. He continued running from the men, howling as he went deeper into the woods. This time the drivers knew the direction he was going and relayed to information to the Sheriff, he then called ahead to let Jim and the Professor know of the change. Jim and the Professor quickly climbed out of the trees and moved in order to intercept the creature to compensate for the change in his direction. They began looking for another place to reposition themselves and wait for him. Not being able to set up in the trees, they waited on the ground in some buck brush.

The two men who had been attacked were okay but were out of action for the rest of the hunt. It would be a couple of days before they would be able to return to their duties. Both of them knew they were lucky to be alive. Being taken to a waiting ambulance, the two deputies were transported to the emergency room for overnight observation. Both of the men were coherent and talking when the Sheriff checked in on them later that night.

The two agents waited in the hospital emergency parking lot as they listened to their radio scanner in their black Escalade. They were waiting for the two deputies to arrive, so they could to talk to both of them about what had happened to them. When the ambulance arrived the agents got out of their vehicle and walked into the emergency room where the hurt deputies were being treated. As they sat and listened to the deputies talk about what had happened they learned about the giant creature that had attacked them. As they listened to them describe the creature to the doctors, one of the agents called the Director about what they had learned from listening to the deputies. The Director smiled to himself as he hung up the phone. Thinking for a moment, he quickly picked it up again and called to have a team dispatched at once to the location of the town, with full gear to take over once the locals caught the beast for them. Within an hour, the team would be on site and ready to take over.

The creature, now moving as fast as he could through the forest, knew it needed time to heal up and recover from the shotgun blasts. He now began searching for a place to hold up where he could go that would allow him time to heal.

The blood trail left by the creature would be easy to follow now. Bill, knowing this, released his dogs, and prayed that he wouldn't lose these dogs as well. The Sheriff and Bill followed the blood trail as the dogs started to bark, letting Bill know they had found the scent to follow. The creature was running scared now and knew if he didn't take time to heal, he would be caught by the dogs and then the men. The shotgun pellets now started popping out of his skin as the healing process had already begun. Still moving deeper into the woods, the blood trail now became less and less. Now it was on the hounds to do their job by staying with the scent of the creature. Still following the sound of the hounds, the Sheriff and Bill kept moving forward, deeper and deeper into the forest.

Crossing a stream, the creature walked up the stream a little ways and then jumping onto some boulders, he continued to do this, moving from boulder to boulder, till he was over onto the other side of the mountain. The dogs getting to the stream, lost the scent of the creature and were not able to pick it up again. Bill and the Sheriff called back on the radio, saying that the trail had gone cold and they didn't know which way to go at this point.

Feeling frustrated, they decided to head back and meet the main body of drivers. The Sheriff called Jim and the Professor to let them know they had lost the trail and were heading back to the valley command post to regroup. Jim, who had heard his call on the radio, was cussing about the loss of the trail and scent, knowing he could do nothing more than head back to the command post as well. With the Professor in tow, they met the main group as they were walking back down the mountain towards the command post. All of them frustrated at being so close to catching the creature and not being able to.

The creature, who didn't hear any more noise, stopped and waited, listening for any kind of noise that would indicate that he was still being followed. Not hearing anything, he found a place to lay down to finish healing up from his encounter with the men. Leaning against a boulder, within thirty minutes he was whole again, still hungry, and ready to eat. Once again, he now began looking for something to eat to sustain himself. Again, smelling the air, he headed deeper into the woods. As he went down the mountain he caught the smell of a campfire and made his way down to where it was coming from. Coming close to the camp, he could see two men who had been fishing, cooking their fish over the fire on a stick hanging between two other sticks. Remembering his last experience of dealing with men, he waited until the men went inside their camper before approaching the fire. Grabbing the fish from the fire he quickly left, and took off out of the camp, eating the fish as he went back up the mountain. When the two men came out of the camper they looked at the fire and not seeing their breakfast of fish, wondered what had happened to them. Looking around, they couldn't see anything out of place, as they stood there looking at each other scratching their heads. Not sure what to do at this point, they ate the eggs and hash browns and put their fishing waders back on, went back to the river to try and catch some more fish for lunch this time.

Calling off the search, everybody headed back into town to try and decide what their next step would be. Jim and the Professor walked into the Sheriff's office, where the Dean and Julie were already seated, they sat down and waited for the Sheriff and Bill to show up as well. As both of them walked in, the Sheriff had his cell phone to his ear, "How are the two that were attacked this morning?"

Listening for a minute he then said, "Well at least that's good news anyway."

Jim and the Professor didn't know about the attack on the two men and were surprised by it. The Sheriff put his cell phone down on his desk and sat down in his chair. He let out a sigh of relief, then looked at Jim and the others, "Well the good news is, my men will recover soon enough. The bad news is, the creature got away from us when he crossed the river, where he is now is anybody's guess."

"I didn't realize some of your men got hurt," Jim said

The Sheriff, shrugging it off as part of the job, asked, "So, how do you want to proceed from here?"

Jim sat and thought about it for a minute or two, not knowing what to do now, "We could continue again like we did this morning, using Bill and his dogs, or we could see if we can track him using a helicopter.

"So far, I've had four deputies get hurt from this creature and I don't know if I can afford to lose any more of them from this point on. So, I'm inclined to see if we can have Bill find the creature for us without the deputies."

"I agree with you Sheriff; do you know the country where he's headed to?"

"A little bit, but I think Bill has been in there more so than I have."

Looking at Bill, both Jim and the Sheriff wanted to know what he thought about it. As he felt their eyes resting on him he said, "The damn thing killed my best two dogs and I want to catch him before he kills somebody. As far as I'm concerned, we can go out this afternoon and search the area again, this time expanding our search past the river for his scent and see if we can pick it up again."

Jim and the Professor agreed with Bill, "The sooner we find him, the greater our chances are of catching him and taking him out of here. The cage is still set up and waiting to be used," Jim said.

"Okay, that being said, we'll go back out this afternoon and all of you will be carrying shotguns and pistols as well."

Getting up from his desk, the Sheriff saw that all of his deputies were standing there, waiting for him in the hallway. He walked out, and he stopped and asked, "What's up men?"

"Well sir, we would like to continue looking for this creature with you sir, the way we see it, if we don't stop him, he'll eventually kill somebody. It's only going to be a matter of time for that to happen, and that somebody could be a family member to one of us," the deputy sergeant said.

Looking at his deputies he asked, "Do you all feel the same way?"

They all shook their heads in agreement, "Either we find him and get rid of him or we, at least, can say that we tried to do it."

"You know I can't pay you guys overtime on this, hell, nobody even knows about this creature. If I have my way, they won't know about it either. That all being said, I could use all of your help on this, and thanks."

"When do we go back out, sir?"

"This afternoon after lunch. Bill will be leading the way back with his dogs, where we lost him this morning. We'll be spreading out from there to find him. After that we'll run him to ground. I think the only way to kill this creature is to cut off its head and separate it from the body."

Jim, hearing the conversation between the Sheriff and his men said, "We will go with our original plan of having drivers push the creature to us. We won't do anything until we find the trail again. At this point in the game, we need to stop this creature anyway we can. If any of you can kill it or we can shoot it with a tranquillizer dart, I don't care at this point, we just need to stop this creature once and for all."

"Once that's done, and we got him, we should be able to handle it from there," the Professor said.

Julie and the Dean, looked at her dad, "We hope we can handle it from there."

Going back out after lunch, they picked up where they left off at the river. Bill, with his dogs, scanned the area, trying to find the tracks and the scent of the creature again. In about forty-five minutes, the dogs started howling after finding the scent once more. All of the drivers came up to where Bill was standing, pointing down at the tracks, indicating that they went downhill, he said, "Here we go again."

The dogs were going to be kept on their leashes while they followed the trail. The deputies would follow Bill until they got close enough to the creature to start making noise again as the drivers. Jim and the Professor, would go out in front again, once they had a general idea of where the creature was headed. Until then, all of the men would stay together until it was time to split up once they had found the creature. The Sheriff thought there was safety in numbers until it was absolutely necessary to split up. Working their way down the mountain, they came across some fisherman at their camp eating a late lunch. Stopping, the Sheriff asked, "Have you guys seen anything out of the unusual, lately?"

One of them said, "Somebody was in our camp and they stole our breakfast this morning while we were in the trailer."

"Did you get a look at who it was, and do you know which way they went?"

"No, not at all, like we said we were in the trailer getting ready to eat breakfast."

The Sheriff told the sergeant to get the men to spread out and start looking over the area around the camp site. In about five minutes, one of the deputies called the Sheriff over, "We think we found something over here, take a look at these prints," the deputy said, as he pointed to the ground.

The fisherman walked over with the Sheriff, who was now looking at the footprints on the ground, "Where in the hell did that come from?"

"You got it right mister, it did come from hell," Jim said.

"I suggest you guys pack it up and get out of here until we tell you it's safe to come back out here," the Sheriff said.

"Do you think he's still out here, Sheriff?"

"If you saw the sheep in the pasture he killed and ate, you wouldn't be asking these kinds of questions. Better yet, are you willing to chance it?"

"I see your point and I don't think we want to."

Bill went ahead of the group with two of the deputies, while one of the deputies assisted the fisherman in getting their stuff ready to go. After the two fishermen left and headed back to town, the Sheriff and the rest of the men proceeded to follow Bill and his dogs once more down the mountain. The trail was easier and all downhill from where they met the fishermen. Bill was making good time with the dogs who were hot on the scent. The creature was nearby, and the dogs could tell now because they were sniffing the air instead of the trail. Bill pulled his dogs back and the deputies had their shotguns at the ready. Standing by for the rest of the team to show up with the Sheriff, Bill and the deputies decided to wait in the clearing opposite the tree line. Having the dogs on their leashes and Bill barely holding onto them, he could sense that the creature was watching them and waiting for the right opportunity to attack.

In fact, the creature was doing just that and couldn't understand why the three men hadn't come any closer to him and were waiting just out of range from him. Being confused by the move of the three men, he waited as well. When the Sheriff showed up with his men and then proceeded to move forward as a group instead of one at a time, this made the creature mad and he let out with a howl to let them know his feelings. The nearness of the yell by the creature surprised all of the men. At this point, all of the deputies had their shotguns at the ready and waiting for the Sheriff to clear them to fire on the creature. By now the Sheriff was on the radio talking to Jim and the Professor, letting them know where they were and asking where he was. Jim acknowledged him, "We're right in front of you guys, let us get closer and see if we can shoot him with our tranquillizer gun."

The Sheriff raised his hand signaling the other deputies to holdup and standby and wait for Jim and the Professor to do their magic. As Jim and the Professor moved closer, they could actually see the creature in the shadows of a stand of trees. The Professor was right behind Jim with his shotgun aiming at the creature's shadow. Jim crept up as the Sheriff made some noise to keep the creature looking in his direction. The creature could tell there were more people in the woods, with all of them being close by, but could not distinguish where each of the smells were coming from. By now, Jim and the Professor were positioned close enough for the shot, which at this range, was going to be easy to do. Pulling the rifle up to his cheek, and finding the creature in his sights, Jim fired the gun. The dart made its way from where Jim was standing directly to the middle of the creature's back, between the shoulder blades. When the dart hit the creature, it let out a scream and came out of the trees, snarling at the deputies and the Sheriff. Turning around and trying to find the dart, he couldn't reach it. The more he tried to find the dart the quicker the tranquilizer started to work. After a few minutes of trying, eventually, he felt the full effects of the tranquilizer, not being able to stand any longer he fell down onto his knees and then fell face first into the forest ground, completely out.

For a few more minutes, nobody moved, waiting to see if the dart had done its job. The veterinarian was the first to come over and check the creature to make sure he was out. Once they were sure, the deputies secured his hands and feet with ropes and wire behind his back. It would take a total of four deputies to lift him by his shoulders and carry him down to where the cage was. All in all, it took about two and half hours to carry him, working in two teams of four men, to get him there. Loading him up into the cage, and posting a guard on the creature, everybody stopped to catch their breath and breathe a sigh of relief after having gotten the creature into the cage. The veterinarian stayed close by with the tranquilizer gun, to keep an eye on the creature in case he started coming to.

The Sheriff, looked at the creature and then the Professor, "Well, we've done our part Professor, what are you going to do now that you've got him?"

"Transport him back to the valley from where he came from as soon as possible. Do you think you might want to come along for the ride?"

"No sir, I feel we've done enough in catching this thing for you, besides I need to go check on my other deputies."

"That you have, and we couldn't have done it without you and your men. We really appreciate all that you've done for us," Jim joined in on the conversation.

"Not that I want this creature away from here, but when do you think you will be ready to go?" the Sheriff asked.

"As soon as we can find out how long the tranquillizer will work on the creature. I think once we can figure that out, the trip should be a cinch," Jim replied.

"Knock on wood," Julie added to the conversation.

As the Sheriff and Jim were talking, one of the deputies came over to them, "The creature is coming to and he doesn't look to excited about being in a cage."

The Sheriff, Jim, and the others, walked over to the cage and watched the creature as it started coming to. Realizing for the first time that his hands and feet were bound together and that he was in a cage. All he could do was lay on the ground, twist around, and howl. It looked as if the restraints on his hands and feet were going to hold him for the time being. The Sheriff, looking at his watch said, "Approximately three hours for the sedative to work before hitting him again with another dose."

The veterinarian loaded up another dose into the gun and fired it once again into the creature to sedate him again. This time the dose was stronger and would last longer than the first one.

At this time, the vet made sure there would be plenty for the trip to the valley.

Jim, looking at the creature, couldn't help but feel sorry for him, not because of the damage he caused, but for being in the wrong place and at the wrong time of history. As he stood there, Julie could sense from Jim what he was feeling, "Don't feel too sorry for him, if he got a half a chance, he'd kill you in a heartbeat and wouldn't think twice about it."

Jim hearing this, nodded and went over to the Sheriff, "I need some help in getting this creature onto a truck or trailer to take him back to the valley, have you got anything that we can use that will work for us?"

The Sheriff thought a minute, "I believe we do have something that will work, let me check really quick on it."

Pulling out his cell phone, he called a number he had in his phone, letting it ring for a couple of times, he asked, "Hey Mike, do you have a trailer I can borrow for a couple of days? I'll bring it back when were done with it."

"I have a roll off the trailer system that is closed and rides on its own trailer, it's set up for sixteen thousand pounds, will that work for you?"

"That should do the trick, I think. I'll have two of my men come down and get it from you in about thirty minutes. Will that be good enough for you?" the Sheriff asked.

Looking around the area, the Sheriff called two of his men over, "I need you to go over to Mikes place and fetch the trailer for our friend in the cage."

The two deputies nodded their heads and took off, getting into one of the cruisers and headed for Mike's place to go get the trailer.

"We'll have it here for you shortly," the Sheriff said, looking at Jim.

Jim nodded to the Sheriff, "I'd better get my people together to start making plans for the trip back to the valley then."

Looking around for Julie, he waved at her to get her attention, "Hey Julie, see if you can find your dad and the Dean and let them know we should be ready to leave here soon and head back to the valley."

Julie nodded, and went to look for her father and the Dean to tell them to get ready to go. Finding them she passed on the message from Jim.

"Can you keep an eye on our friend here while we go get our gear from the motel rooms? It shouldn't take too long, and we'll be back to take him off of your hands," Jim asked the Sheriff.

"Not a problem, but hurry just in case the creature gets homesick for you guys."

"Will do," Jim said as he ran into Julie on his way to the truck. Both of them leaving together to go back to the motel room. The Professor and the Dean met up with them at the Jeep, as well, and went with them to get their stuff ready for the trip back to the valley.

As they got into the Jeep the Dean said, "Now comes the hard part of getting back to the valley in one piece."

"I have a question, how are we going to get the creature over the hiking trail that we take to get to the valley ourselves?" the Professor asked.

Jim sat there for a minute, not having given any thought to that question until now and looked at the Professor, "You picked a hell of a time to bring that question up, you know that don't you?"

Everybody laughed, including the Professor, as he looked somewhat embarrassed by the Jim's reply. "Well I was just thinking about it," he said.

"Actually, it's a good question and one that I hadn't even given any thought about till now that you mentioned it. I was more focused on getting the creature captured than anything else," Jim said.

"Well step one is accomplished and now step two just needs to be figured out," Julie added.

"I wonder if there is an old dirt road that leads to the valley that we can use the truck to get to," the Dean inquired.

"We'll need to stop at the BLM office and see if there is a map showing the trails inside that area of Colorado," Jim said, as he started the truck and drove to the motel to get their gear and check out.

After getting the rooms cleared of their belongings and checked out, Jim and Julie looked at each other, "We need to tell the family about what we've done."

"I think that's a good idea, just for her peace of mind."

The Dean and the Professor stayed in their truck while Jim and Julie went over to the room of the family. They knocked on the door and one of the kids answered it. Julie, looking down on the girl asked, "Are your parents in?"

"Just a minute, mom it's for you," she said, as she waited at the door for her mom to show up.

When the mother approached the door she asked, "Can I help you?"

"You probably don't remember us, but we talked to you not to long ago about your experience at your house."

"Yes, I remember you now, what can I do for you?"

"We thought we'd let you know that we captured the creature today and were taking him out of here to a safe place. Where you won't have to worry about him anymore."

You could see the relief in her eyes when Julie said that, and you could tell it had been on her mind for quite some time. She asked, "I can hardly wait to tell my husband, what happened, how did you catch it?"

"Well, we tracked the creature on one of the mountains up there and shot it with a tranquillizer gun. Once we had it sedated, we captured it, hogtied it, and put it inside a big bear cage to take back with us," Jim said.

"That's good news for everyone around here, did anyone get hurt?"

"Other than the two deputies initially, no one got hurt, fortunately, and now we're on our way to take him back to where he came from."

"I hope it's far away from here."

"It is ma'am, far from here. Well, we best be going now. We felt you deserved to know before we left town," Julie said.

"I'm glad you told us, I'll be able to sleep at night now and maybe go home once it's built again."

"Yes ma'am."

By now Jim was heading back to the Jeep as Julie said their goodbyes to the lady and her daughter. Jim waited in the Jeep till Julie got there and then shifted the Jeep into gear to go meet the deputies who were getting the bear cage. The Professor and the Dean followed them in their truck with the intentions of hooking the bear cage on the back of the Professor's pickup for the creature to ride back in.

As they were leaving town and headed to the camp where the Sheriff was waiting for them, they were stopped by a couple of black Escalades, that were being driven by some government types wearing black suits and sunglasses. Pulling over Jim asked, "What's going on," to one of the men from the Escalade.

"We need to see some kind of identification from all of you," the man closest to the driver's window asked.

After handing their identifications out to him, the man reviewed each one.

"Why are you stopping us?"

The man didn't answer the question and nodded his head at the others that were with him. At this, all of the agents inside the two other Escalades got out and circled the truck, pulling their weapons out yelling, "You need to exit the truck with your hands in the air and get down on the ground!"

Jim and Julie, surprised by this, did as they were told, wondering what was going on and why. Getting out of the truck, all of them were lying face down on the ground. Each of them were handcuffed and then were picked up and leaned up against one of the Escalades, and they were patted down for anything that could be construed as a weapon. Once this was done, all of them were loaded into a black Escalade and taken away. One of the men got into Jim's Jeep and adjusted the seat to drive it, and another into the Professor's truck, they both followed the other Escalades as they left the street. Sitting inside the vehicle, Jim kept asking, "Where are you taking us, why are you doing this?"

The driver didn't say a word in reply as he continued driving. By now the Professor looked at Jim, "It won't do any good asking your questions, they're not going to tell you or us anything at all."

The agent in the passenger's side of the Escalade made a call on his cell phone, "We got the professors with us now. Proceed to step two of the plan."

Jim sat still for the rest of the ride, not saying another word for the duration of the trip. He was mad as hell for what the agents were trying to do. He figured that they had been stopped by what looked like some kind of government agents. As the trip went on, they each knew they weren't anywhere near the site of the creature. With the windows blackened out, they had no idea where they were headed at this point.

While the Sheriff was waiting for the bear cage to show up a fleet of black SUV's came up. The leader of the group flashing his badge at the Sheriff said, "Were taking over this site and I want to thank you for your work in catching this creature for us. We need you to please leave the area, NOW."

The Sheriff, recognizing the government agents for what they were said, "You're welcome and will be leaving now."

The agents had a truck like the one the Sheriff had asked for and their team started moving towards the creature to load him up into their carrier. The vet was talking to the lead agent, "I just sedated him again, he should be out for another two hours at least."

"Thank you for your assistance and thank you for the update, we'll take it from here now," the leader said.

Nodding to one of the men in a lab coat with a vile in his hand, the leader said to the man, "Your job is to keep him asleep until we get back to the complex. You got that doctor?"

"Yes," the doctor said, as he called his own team in to watch over the creature.

The Sheriff, watching all of this, called his men to follow him back to town. The lead agent looked at him, "Of course this never happened, you understand that don't you?"

The Sheriff nodded his head and got back into one of his own vehicles and left the scene. As he drove away, thinking to himself, *I hope Jim and his friends got away.*

At this point he could only guess they did. Calling on his police radio to the deputies that went to go get the bear cage he said, "Cancel the cage and tell Mike thanks for offering it to us."

Getting back into town, the Sheriff contacted one of the deputies that was patrolling the town, "Did anything unusual happen here while we were gone?"

"As a matter of fact, a couple of government vehicles showed up and took the professors with them to who knows where."

All the Sheriff could do now was wonder what was going to happen to the professors and the creature. He, however, was happy that it was no longer his problem.

Chapter XI

The trip in the suburban was especially quiet, with no one saying a word the whole time. The ride took about two hours and they only stopped once to take the handcuffs off to let everybody go to the bathroom. The agents went with the group and stood outside the doors waiting for them to come out of the restrooms. By now it was dark outside and the only thing they could see was the highway they were driving on through the front windshield. Jim caught the sign for the Peterson Air Force Base exit as the driver made the turn. After that, the trip was back up into the mountains. Jim could tell it was getting cooler by now and the pine trees could be seen from the headlights of the Escalade as it drove along the mountain road.

Stopping once at a gated building, one of the agents from the lead vehicle did all of the talking for the Escalades to pass through the gate. Entering into a cave or tunnel, they continued to drive for another ten minutes until they stopped at a place where there was a big door sitting on heavy duty coiled springs. Getting out of the

Escalade, they were led by one of the agents into the opening, past the big door on springs and taken down a corridor to another small room. Each of them were issued a badge to wear. Then again, being led to another room which turned out to be a conference room. Coming through the door, each of them were asked to sit down at the table. One of the agents removed the handcuffs as they took their seats. As they sat there, Jim counted two guards at each of the doors that led into the conference room. Jim looking at Julie and the others and could see that they were all nervous as they waited for whoever called the meeting to show up.

Within minutes the main leader came in with two men acting as bodyguards with him. Looking around the conference table he said, "I'm sorry for so much secrecy and having you brought here. But believe me it was for your own good."

"How do you figure that?" Jim asked

"Well perhaps after we show you this and what we know, maybe you'll understand better."

Nodding at one of the men in the back of the room, the lights went low and a DVD player, that was mounted into the ceiling, turned on. The DVD player played an old film that showed people milling around in a small town in the desert. As the film played the speaker said, "About twenty-five years ago we came across this town that you are looking at. The population was about three thousand people who were farmers and small business owners that supported the town. For all practical purposes, it wasn't much of a town, none the less, the people who lived there were content being there"

In the film, you could see people walking around the town center, driving down main street, and doing the normal day to day stuff, as usual. The film stopped and then another picture came up showing the town completely lifeless. As the camera panned the town, it focused on the bodies of some of the people laying on the ground. Each of their bodies had been ripped apart and pieces of the bodies were laying all over the street. Jim and the others all looked at the speaker for a minute, "What happened to them?"

"I know your questions already, wanting to know what happened to the town and the people that lived there. I will answer your questions but please continue watching."

As they continued looking at the other slides that came up, each one was bloodier that the last one. Some of the bodies had been dismembered and others were gutted, and for the next ten minutes the pictures continued. Now the lights came back on and the slide show was over. As each of them thought about what they had seen in the pictures they were silent. Jim was the first to ask, after a moment of silence, "What happened to the people?"

"Each of them were killed and partially eaten by something that left footprints on the desert floor and in town as well. The town was left deserted forever with no one coming back to claim anything."

"What has that got to do with us?" the Professor asked.

"Well for one thing, you have a live creature, which we have never been able to find or get hold of."

"But that still doesn't answer the question for us though," Jim kept pressing.

"We believe that the town was wiped out by something along the lines of what you found in the forest. And we need to study it to find out all we can about it."

"You don't want to do that," Jim said.

"Why not?"

"You're probably right that they wiped out the town, but you're dealing with something you don't understand and it's more dangerous than you think," Jim replied.

"You can't kill this creature and, in the end, it will kill you or someone else," the Professor said.

"I don't know about that, you were able to stop him," the Director said.

"Only for a little while, not completely though, he's still alive and we can't kill him," Julie added.

"I think with the resources we have here, we can handle it."

Realizing they were wasting their time talking to the Director, the team just sat there not knowing what to say at this point. Knowing it would be their lesson to learn from, they didn't ask any more questions. Jim looked at the Director, "It's your funeral."

"Yes, it is, I thank you for capturing a live one for us. Do you know where it came from?"

None of the team answered the question and just sat there and looking at the Director.

"So, what about us now that you've got the creature what do you need us for now?" the Dean asked.

"We need your silence about this, we need you to tell no one about it and what we are doing here."

"If that's all, you've got it. And by the way what are you doing here?" Jim asked.

"There is one more thing we need to show you before we let you go."

At this point the briefing was over and the Director of the group motioned to the door he had come through, "Please follow me."

As the guards escorted the group down a flight of stairs to another bigger room, one of the guards open the door and all of them walked inside. The room was setup as a huge research area, of sorts, where more of the giant skeletons were laying on the examination tables, with a team of scientists working on each skeleton. As the Director was speaking, telling them about the work they were doing here, Jim saw another door and, when nobody was looking, he opened the door and walked in. Inside the room he saw other giants in large glass containers filled with water and hoses running to and from the glass tubes to a bank of computers that lined the wall of the room. The creatures were moving inside the containers, each with a breathing tube hooked to their faces. Jim couldn't believe his eyes; these creatures were alive and were able to move inside the glass containers. Some of the creatures were babies and others were full grown, with others in between. The creatures that were in the tubes were all different, some had two heads, others had horns, one eye instead of two, others with three eyes. Seeing this, he hurried back through the door and became a part of the group once again. Jim stood there for a minute listening to the Director before speaking, "So all you have found are the skeletons of these creatures?"

"Yes, I'm afraid so, we want to learn what killed them seeing as how they lived for hundreds of years."

"What are you going to do once you figure that out?" the Dean asked.

"The implication for our own people is what we're trying to figure out. If we can find out how they lived so long, we may be able to do the same for people who have cancer and other diseases as well."

"Maybe we need not be playing with this kind of technology," the Professor said.

"I agree with you, until it's one of your kids or grandkids that has cancer or some other type of incurable disease."

Jim put his hand on the Professor and gently squeezed his arm. The Professor looked at Jim for a moment and then saw Jim's eyes. After that no more questions were asked from the group. Jim looked around, "Can we go home now? We all have classes to prepare for this next semester."

"Sure, all we need you to do is sign nondisclosure statements to protect us and what we're doing here. Then we will take you back to your vehicles and you'll be free to go."

Jim and the others were led from the research room back to the conference room where the paperwork was already laying on the table waiting to be signed. Jim signed his paper first and his co-harts were surprised by this. As each one of them signed the paperwork they were all led away back to the black Escalades and loaded back up into them. Being driven out of the complex and to the first gas station, they were dropped off where they found their vehicles waiting for them. As they got out of the Escalade they walked back to the truck and the Jeep. Getting into their respective vehicles, they waited and watched the Escalades leave in the darkness. Once they were gone, Jim got out of the Jeep and crawled around underneath the vehicle looking for anything that didn't belong there. After a minute of looking, he found that the brake lines had been cut and a tracker had been put on the Jeep inside the fender well. With everybody watching what Jim was doing, and wondering what was going on. He got up, then went to the Professor's truck next, and raising his finger to his lips, he motioned for the Dean and the Professor to get out of the truck. Following his lead, they got out and went in to the convenience store. Jim getting down on all fours again, continued to look the truck over, just as he had done on the Jeep, found another tracker, but this time, the brake lines hadn't been cut. Looking around the parking lot, he found an eighteen-wheeler nearby and, without anybody noticing him, put the tracker on the truck. In a couple of minutes, the semi-truck driver came out, got into his truck and drove off into the night.

Gathering everybody together, he explained what he had seen in the other room. He also showed them the cut brake lines under the Jeep and told them about the trackers he found under both vehicles.

"I'm not surprised that they planted bugs on each of our vehicles," said the Professor.

"From the looks of it, we were not meant to be going back to Utah on this trip," Julie said.

"I believe they are building an army of giants that is indestructible and, when shot, can heal without dying," Jim said.

"A good idea, but not with these kinds of creatures. The question is, what do we do about it now?" the Dean asked.

"Well, we get the Jeep fixed first thing in the morning and then we figure our next move from there. I don't like being lied to and having someone try to kill us." Jim said.

All of them agreed with his sentiments and from there they found a motel nearby and spent the night in Colorado Springs, waiting for the morning to find a mechanic to fix the Jeep. Sleeping in till sunrise was what all of them needed, and as soon as the sun was up Jim looked through the yellow pages to try and find a brake specialist to fix his vehicle. Driving carefully over to the brake shop, they took the vehicle in and had the mechanic replace the cut lines on it. After bleeding the brakes to purge the air in the brake system, the Jeep was good as new. With the Jeep back to normal and the team ready to go, they loaded up the stuff they had brought in for the night back into the Jeep and went to breakfast. The only question on their minds at this point was, what do we do now about being set up and them trying to kill us to keep their secret. Jim spoke first, "I don't know about you, but I don't like being lied to, and I don't like being setup to die."

"The question is what do we do about it, we don't dare go to the police about it, and we can't stay here either," Julie said.

"If they find us alive, they could try to kill us for sure. Maybe we should go back to our friend, the Sheriff, maybe he has an idea of what to do," the Professor said.

As each of them considered what the Professor said, all of them agreed with him. After breakfast, they headed back to the Sheriff's office, hoping to be able to figure out their next step from there. By noon, they parked in the front of the Sheriff's building. Walking into the office, they started looking for the Sheriff and, finding him there, he was surprised to see them.

"So what brings you back to our little town? Don't tell me you had a run in with same guys we did?"

"We weren't sure where to go so we thought maybe you could help us," Jim said.

"First of all, what happened to you guys after you left?"

"We were stopped, handcuffed, loaded into a black Escalade, and driven to Colorado Springs for an interesting meeting with some guy we've never seen before. Then forced to sign non-disclosure agreements before we could leave. Then they put trackers on our vehicles and tried to sabotage our Jeep by cutting the brake lines on it."

"Yeah, don't feel too bad, they showed up at the camp where we had the creature locked up in the cage, and basically took him from us, then saying that they were never here."

"We think they are using the creature to create a super soldier to fight wars where the soldier never dies in combat," the Professor added.

"I wondered why they were so interested in our friend, now it all makes sense."

"What can we do about it?" Julie asked.

"From where I'm sitting, basically nothing. If you go after them they'll finish what they started. And if you go back to the college, they'll come and get you there as well. If you tell the world what you know and have seen, they have your non-disclosure agreements and they can throw your backsides in jail for saying anything about it."

After thinking about the options laid out before them Jim said, "It looks as if we're totally screwed, aren't we?"

The Sheriff nodded his head yes adding, "No matter what you do you're supposed to be dead from some freak accident involving your Jeep."

"Then I guess we need to go back to where they took us and get some hard proof of what they are doing and then tell the world about it."

"I believe you are right on that one, otherwise, for all practical purposes, you don't exist anymore. It's hard to make a living when you're supposed to be dead. That all being said, do you realize what you're going up against?"

"Gee, I always thought the government was our friends and were here to help us," the Professor said with a sarcastic tone in his voice.

"Oh, but they are, they're here to help themselves to whatever they want from us and then some. I wouldn't be surprised that they may be looking for you now as we speak, seeing as how no one has reported an accident yet," the Sheriff replied.

"So, what do we do now that we are here? We have no place to go without being caught?" Julie asked.

"It just so happens that I have a cabin up in the mountains you can stay at for a couple of days, mind you, if they find out that I helped you in any way, my job is done just like yours. So please be careful and don't get caught. And be careful how often you use your debit and credit cards they may be tracking them as well."

"We'll do our best not to use them anymore than necessary," Jim said.

After getting the directions to the cabin and paying cash for some extra food at Wal-Mart, they headed to the cabin. Getting there was easy and being off of the main road made it easy to stay out of sight. The cabin was set up on a hill that could be seen, only if you knew where to look. The view from the cabin was excellent for watching the surrounding areas, especially the roads leading in and out of the area. Getting settled into the cabin was easy. It was about one thousand square feet in size, with a porch on the front of the cabin, with a rocking chair sitting on it. There were two rooms inside the cabin, one was the bathroom and the other had two beds in the corner, along with the kitchen and a small dining area in the center of it. Unloading the truck of their sleeping bags and other gear, the place was set up and ready to live in, in about thirty minutes. The Professor and Julie had the first shift for cooking, while the others would do the clean up afterwards. In the meantime, while Julie and her dad started preparing the food, the Dean and Jim went looking for some firewood to start a fire for cooking. In all, the time from starting a fire and cooking the meal only took about one hour. The food wasn't baked beans, much to Jim's delight, but was chicken tenders with fried hash browns.

When dinner was over, and the dishes were done, and everyone was gathered around the table, Jim asked, "So how do we want to proceed with going after the creature and getting our lives back?"

"First off, we need to know where they got him," the Professor said.

"I think that's the easy part, it's in Cheyenne Mountain, close to Colorado Springs," the Dean said.

"What makes you say that?" Jim asked.

"I've seen the pictures of it before and I recognize the door that we passed through. Plus it's a military complex guarded by the United States Air Force. I recognized the uniforms the sentries were wearing."

"If that's the case, getting in there isn't going to be easy then," Julie replied.

"It could be hard if we don't plan accordingly. It just so happens I have a friend that works in there," the Dean said.

"You do, who is he or she?" Jim asked.

"It's a she, and she was one of my students a few years back before she changed her major from archeology to geology. She has her own office inside the mountain and has been asking me to come visit her since she got the job in Colorado at the Cheyenne Mountain Complex."

"When can you set it up for us to go?"

"I think she will be able to see myself and one other person. Basically, you need to decide who is to go with me and who stays behind."

"I suggest the Professor go with the Dean to see his friend. I think they know who I am because of all the questions I asked while we were in there before," Jim said.

"Jim and I will drive the Jeep to the tunnel entrance and wait for you until you're done," Julie added.

With that plan in mind they decided to drive back down to Colorado Springs and have the Dean meet up with his friend and see if they could go in and see the complex. Once inside, they would take pictures of what was inside the one room and, hopefully, the room with the live creatures inside it as well. This all hinged on the fact that they hadn't been found out yet. They all knew that this plan was slightly crazy. Jim thought, and was hoping, that no one would expect them to come back to try and break in to get the proof they needed to reclaim their lives. For the time being, they would stay at the cabin and enjoy the fresh mountain air and the serenity of being in a cabin in the mountains for the night.

Later that evening Jim and Julie were sitting out on the porch looking at the stars, deep in thought about the all that they had been through over the last couple of days. Julie smiled, "Just think, I thought that being a professor at a college was going to be boring and humdrum, but nooo, here we are running from the government, trying to save ourselves from the bad guys."

Jim chuckled, and looking at Julie smiled, "Come on now, you know you love the adventure of life and death situations we find ourselves in."

"Yeah right, I like it better in the books I read, not in real life."

The Professor, overhearing the conversation, looked out onto the porch, "Come to bed kids, we have a big day tomorrow."

Chapter XII

Before leaving the next day, Jim left a note thanking the Sheriff for the use of the cabin signing it, your friends. All of them then loaded up into the truck and the Jeep and headed back to Colorado Springs, looking for the turnoff they had taken earlier with the agents. Finding a motel for their stay in the city, they dropped off all of their stuff and went looking to find Cheyenne mountain. The signs for the Cheyenne Mountain Complex were easy to find. Once they figured it out they drove back into town and had the Dean call his friend to see if it was possible for him to meet with her for dinner. The Dean's friend didn't answer her phone when he called so he left a message on her phone saying he would call her back at six o'clock that evening.

To kill some time, they all decided to see the sights of the area. The zoo was open, and the Garden of the Gods was open as well. By the end of the day, they had experienced both places and all of them were tired and ready to stop for the evening. Dropping Jim and Julie off at the motel, the Dean and the Professor left to make the second phone call. At six o'clock the Dean called again, and this time his friend was home. After being invited to her home, they stayed for dinner and a good conversation about where everybody was at in their careers and what they had been doing with their lives since meeting last. After clearing the table and putting the dishes in the dishwasher, they all retired to the front room and sat down to continue their visit.

"So, what brings you here from the promised land?" Ann asked smiling.

"I decided to take a break in between semesters at the University and take you up on your offer to come see where you worked."

"That shouldn't be a problem, when would you like to see my digs?"

"I don't want to impose, but I was hoping maybe tomorrow would be alright? If it's okay with you, I don't want to create any problems for you."

Ann sat there for a moment thinking, you could see her going through schedule in her head, "How about tomorrow around three o'clock?"

"That would be fine, are you sure it will not be a problem for you?"

"Oh no not at all, I should be done with all of my meetings by noon to catch up on my e-mail, so three o'clock will be fine. I will have a badge for you and your friend, Professor Wainwright, waiting for you at the visitor's center when you get there. Make sure you check in there first, otherwise, they get a little nervous about strangers."

The Dean looked at his watch, "We should be leaving now so you will be ready for us tomorrow. Thank you again so much for dinner and we'll see you tomorrow afternoon."

"It will be my pleasure to show you around the complex tomorrow. I'm so glad you stopped by."

"Till then."

Hugging her goodnight, and leaving the house, the two of them got into the truck and headed back to the motel to find Jim and Julie watching the TV on one of the beds in the room. Opening the door with the second key, the Dean told them it was a go for tomorrow to visit the complex. Jim and Julie seemed relieved by the news and then started stressing out all over again, worrying about tomorrow if something should go wrong.

The Professor, looked at them, "Whatever happens tomorrow, it will be alright."

Jim, Julie, and the Dean all said, "Amen brother," laughing as they said it.

The next day everyone was awake and ready to go, when by chance Jim looked out the window of the motel room and saw a black Escalade sitting in the parking lot of the motel. Sensing something wasn't right about it being there, Jim told everybody, "I think our friends are back. "

The Professor went to the window and looked at the vehicle, noting that it had a government license plate on it, "I believe you're right."

"What do we do now?" Julie asked.

"I've got an idea, I need you two to go down to the front desk and walk out the front doors. I'm going to sneak out through the side door and take care of their vehicle. But I need you to take your gear and load it up into the back of the truck as if you're getting ready to leave, to keep their attention. Can you do that for me?" Jim said.

"You want us to distract them from what?" the Professor asked.

"From me and what I'm doing. Dean, I need you to gather all of our stuff together and get it ready to load in the truck as well but have it ready and waiting on the back side of the motel for when Julie and the Professor come around to get you. Stay inside until you see them coming, do you understand. I'll meet you at the door once I get done doing my part."

At this point, Jim was looking at some of the groceries they had bought from Wal-Mart, finding a small apple and looking at it, said to himself, "This should do the trick, I think."

As Julie and the Professor gathered their stuff, Jim said give me five minutes to get down to where I need to be and then move out as if nothing is wrong. Julie and the Professor, still not sure what was going on, nodded their heads in agreement and proceeded to go down to the front of the motel. Jim left at the same time and was gone just as fast, watching the two men in the black Escalade from the side door. When Julie and the Professor walked out into the parking lot one of the men inside the Escalade nudged the other man with him. Both of them were now watching Julie and the Professor as they walked to their truck. Jim, slipping out of the motel side entrance, came up from behind the Escalade, hiding in between the other cars and slowly made his way to the back of the Escalade. He crawled under the back of the vehicle, took the apple and stuck it into the tail pipe of the Escalade and did a duck walk back to the hotel side door, without being seen.

The Professor got into the truck and started it up and pulled out of the parking lot and headed around to the other side of the motel. The driver in the Escalade went to start his vehicle but it wouldn't start. He kept cranking on the ignition switch, but nothing happened. By now the truck, with the Professor and Julie in it, was on the other side of the motel, stopped to pick up Jim and the Dean with the rest of their gear and drove off, leaving the black Escalade in the parking lot, unable to start. As they drove away, both of the agents were out of their vehicle with the hood up, trying to figure out what had happened to their vehicle.

After a few minutes of driving, Jim had the Professor drive to another motel that was further down the highway and not so close to the motel they had just left. Jim got out of the truck, walking to the corner of the new motel, stood and watched, looking up and down the road for the Escalade. After watching for several minutes, he didn't see the Escalade following. Getting back into the truck the Dean asked him, "What did you do to their Cadillac?"

"I did what any college student would have done to keep the police from catching you. I put an apple in their exhaust pipe, so they couldn't start their Escalade to follow us."

Julie looked at him, "When did you learn to do that?"

"Believe me you don't want to know, it might change your opinion of me of being a good boy."

"I believe you're right about that. The things you learn about your husband after you're married to them for a while."

The Dean and the Professor laughed at the conversation, "It's a good thing she doesn't know about our days of being students, isn't it?" said the Dean.

"I don't remember anything about any of that, leastwise, none that I care to have used against me in a court of law," the Professor said, still chuckling.

"Amen brother, amen."

The ride to the next stop wasn't for another thirty minutes, and only as they headed into the mountains towards Pike's Peak, did they stop for the first time. All of them realized that staying in a motel or hotel was not an option anymore. They would need to camp out until they could get back into Cheyenne Mountain to get the pictures they needed showing what was going on inside.

By now the feds had showed up at the motel after the agents had called in saying that they were having problems with their vehicle.

Arriving at the motel, they picked up the two stranded agents and left behind another junior agent with the Escalade, that had quit on them, to wait for the tow truck. They then headed off down the road to find the truck with the people from Utah, searching the highway and every motel along the way. Their only problem was where to look for them, now that they had been spotted. The Director of the group was upset that the professors from Utah had gotten away from them. He knew that if they told anybody about what was going on inside the mountain it could spell disaster for the project he was in charge of. He had to stop them before they would destroy his work, the work that had meant so much to him, and had the potential of saving so many lives.

The creature now found himself inside a bigger cage, one that was in a sound proof room where no one could hear him scream and howl. A new team of doctors now watched the creature, from behind a bullet proof glass, with a renewed interest of having a live specimen to evaluate and run tests on. The cage was set up in an airtight chamber that could be pumped full of sleeping gas to knock out the creature in order to get blood samples from him to do the toxicology, genetics testing, and lab work. Their main interest was to try and figure out how the creature could heal itself so quickly. The ones in the test tubes were developed from DNA pieced together from the skeletons they had picked up along the way from well-meaning people who turned them into the Smithsonian for display. The others in the test tubes were alive, but were lacking the traits the live creature had and would die if let out of their water tanks, no better than fish in a larger aquarium. For all intents and purposes, the creature they had taken from the professors, was no better off than when he had been caged alive 3,000 years ago in the valley in central Colorado. Being fed by his captors and cared for, more out of fear than anything else, living out his days in the valley, eventually being killed or dying from old age. Here in the laboratory, in the mountain, nothing had really changed for the creature, all of this was being done in the name of science for the good of man in the time of war.

Finding a camping spot off the beaten trail, the team set up camp once more and made themselves comfortable for the time being. As they started to set up the camp site Jim said, "I got to tell you, I'm getting tired of sleeping on the cold hard ground anymore. Why, I remember when this used to be fun, but not anymore."

They all shook their heads in agreement as they ate their lunch and waited for the time to meet with Ann at the Cheyenne Mountain Complex. Until then all they could do was try to rest, relax, and keep an eye out for anybody that might find it unusual for them to be camping there. Around two o'clock they headed back down the mountain and went towards the Cheyenne Mountain Complex.

Driving up the canyon and parking near the gate where the visitor center was, the Professor and the Dean exited their truck and walked to the visitor control center to get their badges. When they were cleared they walked into the tunnel where another vehicle was waiting for them and drove them to the door of the complex. Ann was waiting for them at the entrance and after greeting her friends with a hug offered to start the tour. Both the Dean and the Professor were impressed with the size of the complex and the purpose behind it. The original plan for it being built was for use during the cold war as a command center for Missile defense and space track for all of North America. Being inside a mountain it could withstand a direct strike from a nuclear weapon and still be a central command

and control for any threat from Russia and the Warsaw Pact Nations. As time went on their mission was expanded to include the southern hemisphere from third world country threats who had acquired a nuclear capability.

Ann went on about her job being needed in the complex to keep check on the rock structure of the mountain that housed the complex, was at best, exciting when the seasons changed and the effect it had on the mountain as a whole. The seasons would stretch and shrink the rock surrounding the complex which brought its own set of problems for the geologist to work out so as not to affect the mission of the complex.

As they made their way through the complex, the Dean recognized one of the conference rooms from their previous visit the other night. "Is there anything else that that's going on in here besides the missile defense for the nation?" he asked Ann.

She looked at the Dean with a serious look on her face, "None that I'm aware of."

"I was just wondering about some of the stories and rumors I've heard about it being a medical place for nontraditional studies."

"I'm not aware of anything like that going on," Ann replied.

The Professor looked down a hallway, "What's down this way?"

"Well, I don't really know; this place is like a honey comb with all of its mazes. You almost need a map to know where you need to go around here and to keep from being lost."

As they continued walking down the hallway towards the door at the end of the hall, Ann tried the handle and found it was locked. The Dean, looked at her, "Would you believe me if I told you that behind that door is a big room full of medical equipment being used for the study of creatures that have been dead and gone for over three thousand years?"

Ann smiled at him for a second, thinking he was joking, but when she saw he wasn't smiling and that he was serious about what he had said and noticing that the Professor wasn't smiling either asked, "How do you know this?"

"Well, it started off as a quest to find a creature from a valley in central Colorado… and it has led us to here after they took it from us."

After explaining their story to her she looked at the two of them, "But what does that have to do with being here."

"We were taken to another level inside this complex and shown what they were doing with their science experiments. Then they released us after signing a Non-Disclosure Agreement. That's when we found a tracking monitor and that our brake lines on our Jeep were cut. In fact, they are still looking for us as we speak."

"Aren't you taking a chance being here then, you could get caught being in here?"

"Well, we have no choice, we can't go back to our jobs at the university because they will find us and kill us there in some kind of freak accident. We've seen too much for them to allow us to keep living. We have become what you would call a liability to their agenda."

"A loose end in their plans that needs to be tied off one way or another so that they can continue with their experiments," the Professor added.

Ann, looking at the Dean and thinking about what they had told her, wondered if they could be trusted and finally realizing that the Dean was her friend and not some kind of mad professor said, "You know there is a lot of things going on in this place. People wearing lab coats walking around on some of the other levels that I'm responsible for, but I have never been allowed access to, as it is part of my job for safety inside the mountain. Is that the kind of thing you're talking about?"

"Yes, we are, the problem is, unless we have proof, we can't go anywhere without the threat of them trying to silence us. I know this is hard for you to believe, but we have no choice but to get pictures of what we saw the last time we were here."

"Otherwise, we have no life we can return to without being threatened or our loved ones being threatened, as well," the Professor added.

Ann didn't respond to what both of them had said. As she looked at her watch she replied, "Well, I need to get back to work and you need to leave before they catch you here."

Not saying another word, she escorted them back to the front of the complex and had a driver take them both back to the visitor center. The Professor and the Dean got out of the vehicle and Ann said, to them as she shook their hands, "Well it was good to see you again, don't be a stranger. Come visit me tonight for dinner and bring your handsome friend with you."

The Professor blushed at her comment and smiled, "Thank you for the compliment."

"So, let's make it about six o'clock for tonight?" Ann said.

"That will be fine, until tonight then. Goodbye," the Dean said.

"Goodbye," Ann said as she got back into the vehicle to go back to her office inside the mountain.

They stood there watching as Ann drove back into the mountain until she was out of sight, then the Professor and the Dean got into their truck. The Dean looked at the Professor and said, "Gee I didn't think you had the magic anymore, you sly old dog you."

"I think she is blind in one eye and can't see out of the other eye."

They both laughed as the Professor put the truck into gear and started to make their way out of the parking lot and down the side of the mountain. When they got back to their campsite they found Jim and Julie sitting next to the fire, anxious to hear how their trip went.

"So, how did it go today?" Jim asked first.

"To be honest with you, I'm not sure about it. I think she believed us, but I saw no indication from her about helping us," the Professor said.

"Although, she thinks your dad is handsome and has invited us back for dinner at her place," the Dean added.

"Now, why wouldn't she think my dad is handsome? All of the girls in his class thought he was the bomb, leastwise, that's what mom used to say," Julie said smiling.

Now the Professor turned beat red and looking away, said to himself, "My reputation precedes me," as he chuckled to himself and sat down next to the fire, enjoying the warmth of it as it radiated out.

At five thirty all of them got into the truck and drove down to Ann's house. Jim and Julie got out of the truck a block away to keep an eye on the house from the outside, just in case something went wrong. They stayed out of sight, in the shadows, as they watched the Professor and the Dean go up to the front door step of the house and ring the doorbell. The door opened, and Ann let them inside. Closing the door behind her, they went in and sat down on the couch in the front room while Ann put the final touches together for the dinner that night. Ann seemed her natural self in the conversation and excused herself to go into the bathroom for a second to freshen up a bit. When she came back the conversation picked up again between the kitchen and front room. Ann was pouring the water into the glasses when the doorbell rang. When she answered it, two agents came rushing through the door with their guns drawn and headed into the front room. The two agents, standing over them, had the Professor and the Dean dead to rights. Contacting their team leader, the agent let him know that they had the Professor and the Dean under arrest.

Having the Professor and the Dean raise both of their hands in the air, they led the two of them out of the house. The Dean, looking at Ann, gave her a look of betrayal. She lowered her head, "They caught me this afternoon snooping where I shouldn't have been. But I did see what you claimed was there and it is true what you said. I had no other choice but to go along with them, they threatened me and my family, as well."

Putting handcuffs on all of them they led the three of them out to the parked Escalade in front of the house. The Professor rode in the center with the Dean on one side and the Ann on the other side of the vehicle. Ann reached over and touched the Dean without saying anything, looking into his eyes. He saw her eyes as she begged for forgiveness. The Dean's eyes met hers and he nodded and smiled mouthing the words, "It's okay, I understand."

Jim and Julie watched all of this from their vantage point as the Dean, the Professor, and Ann were being led out of the house and could do nothing but watch. Waiting a few minutes after the team drove off with their friends, Jim and Julie went to Ann's house. Jim broke a window near the front door and was able to unlock the door. He went inside and started looking for Ann's car keys and upon finding them, they got into her car in the garage. Opening the garage, they pulled out of the driveway and started driving the car around, looking for the Escalade to follow back to the complex. Within minutes, they had spotted the Escalade and started following it, staying in the lane next to them so as not to be picked up in the Escalade's rear-view mirror. Once there, Jim parked Ann's car in the visitor parking lot. Watching the guard at the gate, they waited until the gate was open and the guard was busy. Using Ann's badge, the guard was too busy to pay attention to the picture, allowed Julie to drive her car through the gate into the tunnel, while Jim hid in the backseat of the car under a blanket.

The tunnel was poorly lit thereby allowing Jim and Julie to drive through without being noticed. Finding a golf cart, they parked Ann's car and drove the cart to the main door. Parking the cart near some others that were already there, they watched the comings and goings of the people as the guard checked them as they went to and from the access point. The guard was lax in his checking the badges at this point, figuring the first guard had done his job. As a group of people were coming through the door to go home, Julie and Jim snuck in, going past the crowd, blending in with them, were able to get inside the building. As they made their way through the maze of rooms and hallways they looked for something recognizable from their last meeting inside the complex. Finding a room that was unlocked, Jim stuck his head inside and saw that it was the conference room they had been in. Both Jim and Julie quickly went into the conference room and locked the door behind them. They stayed in there for a couple of seconds while trying to reorient themselves to the room, trying to figure out their next move. Once getting their bearings, they headed to the door in back of the conference room. Going through the door they found themselves in another hallway going towards another door. Jim thought to himself, *"This is better than a corn maze in a farmer's field during the fall season."*

Going down the stairs and reaching the door, he opened it cautiously, looking through the crack of the door, he found himself looking inside the room where the skeletons were located. Looking back at Julie he smiled at her, leading the way into the room, and finding the place empty of workers, they started searching for white coats to put on to look more like scientists to fit in, just in case somebody was still there. He walked around inside the room while Julie was putting on her lab coat. Searching the expansive room, they went from table to table looking at each of the skeletons on the examining tables. Jim, looking around the room, found some filing cabinets next to one of the tables. Opening the filing cabinet and searching the files, he found pictures inside one of the folders that had paperwork attached to them, documenting where they had found the skeletons, the dates, and who found them. Realizing there was nothing here of value, they took the files anyway. Jim now started looking for the room where the actual living creatures were located. Finding the door that he had used once before, he carefully opened it. Checking to see if there were people on the other side, and finding none, he went through the door and located the big tubes of water with the creatures inside them. He signaled Julie, "Follow me."

As both of them went through the door into the room, Julie couldn't believe her eyes at what she was seeing. All of the creatures were moving inside the glass tanks, trying to get out but unable to. Jim pulled Julie closer to his side and moved to the side of one of the glass tubes as they were walking around looking at the creatures. One of the creatures, looking at Julie, tried to scream at her but his oxygen masked covered the sound of the scream. Julie stood there, frozen as she looked at the creature. Waiting for a second before continuing. Jim kept moving around the room and finally grabbed Julie by the arm to follow him.

Finding an office in the center of the room, Jim went in and started checking the desks for anything that would get them and their friends out of the jam they were in. Opening one of the bottom drawers of a desk, Julie found a few files inside with pictures of the room where the test tubes were located. Grabbing these and a few other files from one of the other desks, they quickly put them under their lab coats and quickly retraced their steps back to the door that led to the other room where the skeletons were located. Leaving the room where the skeletons were, they made their way to the conference room. From there they made their way back to front where the gate and the guard was posted. Waiting again, Jim gave her the files he had, and started to distract the guard's attention by creating a scene while Julie walked past the guard with her badge showing and left the area. Jim was caught by the guard and he watched as Julie made good her escape. Finding the cart,

Julie drove till she was able to get to Ann's car. Getting in the car, she drove out past the second guard and continued driving out of the complex down to Colorado Springs to the local newspaper office.

When the news reached the Director of the science project that they had captured Jim inside the complex, he was elated. The guard brought Jim to his office and when he opened the door, Jim could see the others sitting on the couch waiting for him. The Director got up from his desk and smiled at all of them, thinking to himself that he had the upper hand now.

"Well, what do I do with you now?" He asked, looking at all of them.

"How about you let us go and we promise we won't say anything about your experiments here," the Professor said.

The Director laughed, "Cute, real cute, but I hadn't given that idea any thought. I was thinking of something a little more drastic for all of you."

"How about you let us go and I won't have my wife drop off the files we picked up in the office, where the live creatures are kept, to the newspaper," Jim said.

The Director looking at Jim smiled, "You're joking you don't have any files."

"Why don't you have some of your men go check out the offices where the files are kept. Where the desks are located and the filing cabinet alongside the examination tables in the first room you showed us the last time we were here."

The Director, looking at Jim, trying to determine if Jim was blowing smoke, reached down onto his desk and hit a buzzer which brought in one of his men, "Go down to the main areas and do a security check on the filing cabinets and the desks in the offices, to see if anything is missing. Please let me know if you find that anything is missing."

The Director smiled and sat down while looking at Jim and waited to find out the news. Jim, looked at the Director, "You'll find that some pictures of the actual tests your running are missing as well as some of the folders from the skeletons."

The Director looked a little more nervous now and didn't say a word as they waited for the security man to come back. Within minutes the man came back, "We've had a security breach in both areas of the rooms."

Excusing the man from his office, the news of the missing files visibly upset the Director. Jim looked at him, "If my wife doesn't hear from me in twenty minutes she will drop the files off at the newspaper office with one of the reporters that work there. Who knows, with any luck the reporter might get some kind of award for his piece about what you're doing here in downtown Colorado Springs. I really don't know for sure, but what do you think?"

The Director thought about what Jim had said, "How about we shoot you four and bury you where they won't find you ever again?"

"Oh, come now, do you really want to add murder to your resume'?"

"I wouldn't do it, but I have people who will."

"Either way, you are done as far as your career goes. Once they find our bodies, which they will after my wife tells them that the last place she saw me was here with my friends, visiting you in your office. What are the chances they'll come looking for you, or better yet, would you like to talk to my wife first?'

Handing the Director his cell phone after dialing the number for him, Julie answered the phone, Jim I've got a reporter here wanting to talk to the Director, what should I tell him?"

Handing the phone back to Jim, "Hang on a second, I'm waiting for the Director to make up his mind right now."

The Director thought about this for a minute, "You are hurting this country by what you're doing, you know that don't you?"

"What are you trying to do to us, our murders justify saving others from dying?" the Professor asked.

"Where does the government find people like you?" Ann asked.

The Director, realizing he was between a rock and a hard place, had no other choice than to relinquish his control over Jim and the others, nodded his head in agreement with Jim. "Okay, you win, for now."

Answering Julie, Jim said, "See if you can find a safe place to store them without any interference and we'll meet you at Ann's house."

"Ok, I'll see you later. By the way, what do I tell the reporter now?"

"Tell him never mind, but get his business card just in case we need him again."

Looking at the Director Jim said, "What you're going to do is escort us to the front of the mountain, past the tunnel. You're going to forget about us and go back to the hole you came from and leave us alone. If you don't, the files will come out in the news, most likely in Utah or New York."

"If anything happens to any of us, the folders with the information will be in a safe place to be opened in case one of us dies," the Dean said.

"You know you won't get away with this, don't you?"

"Are you willing to risk your career on it Director? Come on, let's get moving."

Grabbing the Director by the coat, Jim pushed him into the door and then opening it he yelled out, "Drop your weapons or I'll break his neck right here, right now."

The Director screamed for his men to do as they were told and dropping their guns on the floor, Jim told the Professor to grab the guns and bring them along. The Professor did so and kept one for himself and gave the other guns to the Dean and Ann. Jim took one as well and put it behind the Director's ear, whispering, "Give me a reason to blow your head off."

"Let's go to the lab where you're keeping our friend," the Professor said.

The Director was scared but questioned Jim, "Why do you want to go there and what are you going to do in the lab?"

"Shut up you'll see," Jim said.

As they made their way to the lab where the giant test tubes were, Jim yelled at the other guards to gather round. With the help of the

Professor and the Dean, herded them into the main office and locked the door so no one could get out. The Professor, pulling the phone cord out of the wall, threw the phone onto the ground. After getting that done, Jim, looking at the computer and the test tubes with the creatures inside them, turned to the Director, "I'm kind of perplexed right now, maybe you can help me solve this issue I have. Should I shoot the computer of one or all of the test tubes? I just don't know, what do you think I should do?"

The Director turned white as a sheet, knowing either way it would be years of hard work gone in a matter of seconds, "Please don't, we really are trying to save lives in combat by what we're doing here."

"If that's true, I want you to release our friend, so we can take him back with us to where he belongs."

"What are you talking about, he's the only living creature we've ever found. We can learn more from him than anything else we have in here."

"Well it's like this, we made a promise that we would bring him back with us. We were in the process of doing that when some guys showed up and took him, without even asking us."

"Really poor manners, if you ask me," the Dean said.

The Director, looking at the computer and the test tubes and thinking about the creature, said, "How do I know you won't release the files to the press if we give the creature back to you?"

"Well first off, you don't. I guess you'll have to trust us, won't you? Then again, how do I know you won't come after us once were gone?"

"I guess you'll have to trust us as much as we trust you," the Professor said, sarcastically.

Jim raised his gun to fire at the computer and the Professor raised his gun towards the test tubes and pulling the hammers back on their guns, now looked at the Director, "Call the coin Director, heads or tails."

The Director screamed, "Okay, okay you win!" as beads of sweat started forming on his brow.

Jim and the Professor lowered their guns and put them on safety. Jim, now looking at the Director, said, "This is the place I want you to deliver the creature to," giving him the address and directions on how to get there. "We'll meet you there in two days. Remember, if anything goes wrong, or you double cross us, the files will be delivered to the newspapers."

The Director nodded his head in agreement as he looked at the directions of where to drop off the creature. Thinking a little bit said, "Hey this is in the Royal Gorge country, isn't it?"

"I'll never tell, let's go now," Jim said.

Jim had the Director lead the way to the front of the conference room and followed him, as did the others, to the front gate. The guard, seeing the Director leading the group, let them pass to go to a waiting Escalade to take them to the front of the tunnel of Cheyenne Mountain, and from there to Ann's house.

"Oh, by the way, the escalade that's broken, has an apple in the tail pipe," Jim said as he smiled.

"We found it after doing three hours of diagnostics on the vehicle."

Leaving the complex with the Director in the truck, they made their way to Ann's house. The ride was in the dark and Jim couldn't tell if anyone was following them to her place or not.

Once there, the black Escalade left without the Director in the vehicle. Jim, looking at the Director who was confused, said, "I've changed my mind, you're going with us on our trip."

"Would you like to come in and have something to drink?" Ann asked everybody.

As they walked into Ann's house they made themselves comfortable and sat down at the table. While everybody was seated, the Professor helped Ann with the beverages. Ann looked at the Professor, 'You were wonderful tonight, backing Jim up in his actions."

He looked up at her, "You didn't do too bad yourself in there either."

"So, you think we make a good team working together?"

The Professor leaned over and kissed her, "I think we do, don't you?"

She looked surprised for a second and then, leaning into him, saying as she kissed him, "Is this what you do on all your first dates? If so, I do agree."

"Well, we better get these drinks in there pronto or they might be thinking something is going on in here and start storming the walls here shortly."

Ann laughed and said, as she picked up the tray full of glasses, "Let them."

Julie found herself back at Ann's house and, parking Ann's car in front of the house, called Jim, "I'm right outside the door and will be coming in soon, so don't shoot me."

Jim unlocked the door and let her in and gave her a hug. As he closed the door behind her, they both stood there holding each other. The Director was watching them from the front room and started realizing that these people were being honest and normal. Not like the ones he was used to dealing with, which wanted results not excuses. For the first time in his life he realized how alone he was and how much his work had taken over his life. It was important work, but to sacrifice your own happiness had been a terrible price for him to pay. The laughter coming from everyone was nice to hear, and with them being Mormon, meant it was good clean fun.

As he listened to them talking, he could tell they were not talking about overthrowing the United States government or the constitution. It was about their lives and what they enjoyed about living, their hopes and their dreams. It wasn't about power or political position or anything like it. They were truly happy doing and living their dreams and their ideas of happiness. The Director had forgotten all about the common man and the common ideals that made life worth living. No politics, no charade, or facade, just living life and enjoying it. He had forgotten how life could be fun and enjoyable and it reminded him of a simpler time and place that he had forgotten because of all the demands of his job. Granted, it was important work but not worth sacrificing yourself for it.

With this thought in mind, he realized that these people were not the enemy and that they deserved an opportunity to continue living and maybe, just maybe, they could be trusted in what they were doing in taking the creature back to the valley where he originated from. For the first time the Director truly felt he was all alone in the world with nothing but his work to show the world that he couldn't tell anyone about.

Chapter XIII

The next morning the sun came up six minutes earlier than the day before and the weather was nice and cool for a clear summer morning. The mountains were green with trees and vegetation, adding their colors with the Columbines in full bloom. There was still snow up on Pikes Peak and seeing the mountain reminded them about the gear they had left up on there. The Professor and Ann offered to go get the gear and were quick to get out the door and into the truck before anybody could say anything to them about it.

Julie looked at Jim and they both smiled at her dad, realizing that her dad was still attractive to the opposite sex, and would be considered quite a catch for any lady. Jim smiled as well, knowing that his father in law had been smiling more often lately, than he had before.

Within an hour and a half, both the Professor and Ann were back with the gear from the camp site. While they were gone it was decided that they would leave this morning to head back to the valley of the giants, as they called it. This intrigued the Director and he was starting to get interested in the field trip they were about to take.

"What is this valley of the giants you guys are talking about?" The Director asked Jim.

"I really don't know if I should tell you at this point. All I can say is you'll have to wait and see till we get there."

The Director, looking at Jim said, "You know that my people will be looking for me, thinking that I've been kidnapped by a rowdy gang of malcontents here?"

"For your sake, I hope they don't find us."

"How about I call them and tell them to knock it off, so we can go where we need to without any hassles from anyone."

Jim was surprised by his offering and looking at him shocked, "Alright what's up?"

"Nothing, I was just thinking about now wanting to see where we are going and not having any problems along the way."

"What do you want from us?"

"Nothing, just let me make a phone call and tell my people to stand down till we get to this valley you're talking about going to in order to drop off the creature. You might say my curiosity is piqued."

"Let me think about it and I'll let you know my decision."

"As you wish."

Jim went and talked to the rest of the team about what the Director had said and what he was offering to do. Asking for their opinions, they all were mixed on their reply's. Julie and Ann said not to trust him, the Professor and the Dean were not sure which way to go on their feelings. Jim finally decided, "I think we need to take our chances and just drive to the site."

Not saying anything to the Director except, "I believe we'll take our chances going to the valley of the giants without you calling anyone."

The Director nodded his head, knowing that they would run into his people sooner or later on the trip. By now everyone was loading their stuff back into the truck and Ann's car. There wouldn't be enough room for all of them to ride together in one vehicle, so the Professor offered to drive Ann's car while Jim drove the truck. They would pick up Jeep later when everything was completed, and the creature was in his place back in the valley.

Once everything was loaded and ready to go all of them went to their vehicles and waited for Jim to take the lead. As Jim pulled out to start down the road, two black Escalades pulled in front of them with agents pouring out of the Cadillac with their guns drawn. All of the agents were ready for a fight to the death against Jim and the other kidnappers. The Director seeing this, and knowing someone could get hurt, got out of the truck and walked over to the lead agent and talked to him for a couple of minutes. The Director turned, and looking towards the truck, called Jim out, asking for his gun and then handing it over to the agent said, "I'm going on a trip with these guys to somewhere in Colorado and I'm going willingly with them. I need you to make sure that the creature we took from them is returned to them at this location in two days. We will be waiting for you. Once you have delivered the creature you will return to the office and wait for my return. Are there any questions?"

The lead agent stood there, perplexed and confused, as the Director said his peace and didn't know what to say except, "Yes sir, we will deliver the creature to you as requested."

"If I'm correct, the best way to deliver the creature would be by helicopter."

Jim nodded in agreement, "Yes, it would be the best way for the creature to get there," not sure as to what to say or how to handle the situation any longer.

"Use my helicopter to deliver the creature, make sure he is heavily sedated before you bring him to us. Jim, I think we should be going, don't you?" the Director said, looking at the lead agent.

Jim climbed back into the truck and everybody just sat there, surprised and confused by the Director's actions. Needless to say, the agents were just as surprised as the others, as well. The Director, looking at the agents said once again, "It's alright, I'll be fine, and you just deliver the creature like I said."

"Yes sir, we'll do as you say."

The agents got back into their black vehicles and left the place and drove off. As the Director got back into the truck he looked at Jim, "Let's go, we're burning daylight."

"We are at that," Jim smiled, as he put the truck into gear and started driving down the road looking for Interstate 25.

Accordingly, it would take a couple of hours of driving to get to the Royal Gorge area once again. Jim stopped at the base camp from a previous trip to use it as a reference point to find the right trail to follow. He looked around, and with the assistance of the Professor and Julie, was able to find the right trail. Unloading most of their gear and putting it on their backs to carry, they started up the trail. Being back here for most of them was like old home week. The newbies were wondering just where they were going as they moved, following the others up the trail.

It took a little longer for them, simply because the Director and Ann were not used to hiking and carrying their own back packs up a mountain. The Professor was very attentive to Ann and her needs, while the Jim assisted the Director when needed. By the late afternoon, they had made their way to the campsite by the waterfall and pitched their tents there for the night. Ann and Julie, with the help of the Director and the Professor, prepared the evening meal. As they cooked the food over the open fire the Professor asked the Director, "Why didn't you turn us in when you had the chance to?"

"I realized that you guys were on the square about what you were doing, and when I saw Jim holding his wife Julie, it made me realize that I had no one that worried about me like that, that cared enough to love me. All I have ever had was my job and nothing else really mattered to me."

The Professor, looked at the Director, "Your lucky, you are still young enough to find some happiness out there for yourself."

"I'd say you been lucky twice in your life," nodding at Ann.

The Professor chuckled, "Twice in a lifetime, who would of thought."

Jim was feeling pretty tired from the hike and as he sat down next to Julie started teasing her a little, which for Julie, was getting in the way of her chores. Jim pressed the issue with her and finally, taking the dish clothe and throwing it at him yelled, "If you don't quit messing with me, I swear you'll be sleeping alone tonight and I hope you freeze!"

Jim laughed and threw the dish clothe back at her, "Who's going to protect you from the bears and snakes out there?"

"Ha! I'm not afraid of bears and snakes, but you should be afraid of me, Jimmy boy!"

Everybody laughed at the actions of the two of them. The rest of the night was spent sitting around the campfire talking about all of the adventures they had up to this point. The Director spoke last, "I owe you all an apology for my actions and how I've treated you. I'm so used to dealing with the politics of the job that I naturally thought the same about you all. I was wrong and I'm sorry for my actions towards all of you."

All of them smiled.

"Apology accepted, by the way what is your name anyway?" Jim said.

"My name is Dan Smith and I'm from Bozeman, Montana, and I should be in better shape than I am from having lived up there."

Everybody smiled and chuckled at Dan's comment.

"Glad to have you here, Dan from Montana," Julie replied.

In the dark a voice was heard calling into the camp, "Hey you in the camp, can I come in?"

Jim yelled back at the voice, "Depends, are you friend or foe?"

The voice laughing, yelled back, only closer this time, "Depends, do you have any food left?"

Jim stood up and introduced Red Hawk to the team, as he walked in the camp. The old team remembered who he was, but for Ann and Dan, he was new to them. Shaking hands with everyone Red Hawk looked at Dan, "Have we met before?"

"You do look familiar to me, as well."

"Oh well, it doesn't matter, what's for dinner? I'm hungry enough to eat a bear right now," sitting down next to Dan.

"Well, we have baked beans for dinner and for desert we have baked beans with pineapple on it. I know it's your favorite," Julie said, smiling.

"Well in that case, I think I'll have some baked beans then. Just out of curiosity, are these the same beans from last time you guys were here?"

"I think they are, just aged a little more is all," Jim said, laughing.

"Well how do you like that, they weren't complaining when they were hungry were they, Ann?" Julie said.

"No, they weren't, the fact was, they were happy to have it to eat."

"If they're not careful, they may get it for breakfast as well," Julie added.

"You mean were not having it for breakfast? Man o man, I was sure looking forward to it myself. There's nothing better than a home cooked meal of baked beans from a can over an open fire to start the day off," Jim said, as he laughed.

"Well, I never," Julie said

"Me neither," Ann joined in.

"So, this is how married folk get along now days," Red Hawk said, smiling.

"Who said we were married?" Julie asked.

"Oh, the pain, the hurt, oh what will I do, our first fight over a can of beans?" Jim said, feigning pain.

They all laughed at the two of them.

Red Hawk looked over the camp, "I guess tomorrow is going to be a big day, isn't it?"

"We hope so, leastwise, if everything goes right," Jim said.

"God willing and the river don't rise," The Dean said.

Red Hawk stood up, "Well, I'll see you tomorrow hopefully, bright and early, until then good night."

Everybody said goodnight to Red Hawk as he left the campfire. Both Dan and Ann looked confused, curious as to where he was going so late at night and as they looked towards Jim he replied, "He has a camp out there with his friends in one of the valleys were going to tomorrow."

Ann looked at the Professor, "This is getting real interesting being out here."

"Believe me, you ain't seen nothing yet," the Professor said, as he unrolled his sleeping bag next to Ann's sleeping bag in the tent.

"I'll have to take your word for it."

With that the two of them crawled into their sleeping bags and wished everybody a good night. And soon were fast asleep.

"You and I will be sharing the same tent and I've already put your sleeping bag inside the tent for you. So, when you're ready you'll know where to go to sleep," the Dean said, looking at Dan.

"Thank you very much. If you don't mind, I like to stay out here and look at the stars and the fire for a little while longer."

"Suit yourself, I'm turning in for the night."

Dan had forgotten how peaceful the nights in the mountains could be, seeing the stars reminded him of when he was a boy in Montana growing up. Whatever problems he had, he knew going to the mountains was his sanctuary from them all. Living on the reservation during the summer months was the greatest joy in his life. Sleeping under the stars and staying up to watch the falling stars, till he fell asleep, was one of his best memories. Tonight, he would relive his childhood experiences again for the first time in years. Getting up early to go fishing the next morning was his next favorite thing to do. He had forgotten all about what it was like being a kid because of his job. Now days it was all work and no play, he chuckled to himself, "That is all about to change for me now."

As he sat watching the fire, he wondered about all of his old friends he knew as a kid growing up, *I wonder what they're up to now, and what about Jane, my first love in high school?"* he thought to himself, remembering how she was the prettiest girl in the school.

For the first time, his eyes were wet from the memories of his youth and wiping away the tears, he closed them for just a moment and all the years disappeared all at once. Seeing himself laughing and playing with his friends, it all came alive, as if it were yesterday. He smiled for the first time in years, remembering all of it again for the first time. How he missed his friends and loved ones. He made himself a promise that once this was done he would go home again, to see for himself how things were now. With that, he looked up into the sky, thinking what a fool he had been for forgetting himself and the others who were his friends. "Thank you, God, for reminding me about what is real and worth more than all of the gold in the world," he said, still looking at the stars in the sky.

With that, he turned in for the night. Taking his sleeping bag out of the tent, he crawled into it under the stars and started counting the falling stars once more till he fell asleep. For him It would be the best night's sleep he had had in years, dreaming the dreams of his boyhood years and remembering how much fun it was to be young again.

Chapter XIV

Dan was up early the next morning as he had found a stick and some fishing line and fastening the line to the stick he went to the river to find some worms and try his luck at fishing. The chill was still, there but he felt good about being able to fish and enjoy seeing the sunrise coming over the mountain. In fact, as the sun rose, the rays of the sun played on the river, creating a reflection of shimmering lights on the beach next to him. He marveled at how beautiful it was and how often this happened when no one was here to see it. He was thankful for being here to appreciate it.

While lost in his thoughts he felt a tug on his line and being careful he brought the fish to the surface. Seeing that it was a small fish, he was happy when it spit the hook and dived back down to the bottom of the pool. Dan smiled, "Next time, maybe you won't be so lucky, until then my friend."

Jim, waking up and walking around the camp, saw Dan down by the river. He went down to where he was fishing, "Any luck so far?"

Dan smiled, "I hooked a big one a couple minutes ago and it damn near broke my line," holding out his hands to show how big it was, "It was this big."

"That looks like the one I caught and believe it or not it got away from me, as well," Jim laughed.

"Man, that's one lucky fish, isn't it?"

"I think you're right."

"Well it's time to eat breakfast, if you're interested."

"And miss out on the baked beans for breakfast, not me mister. I just about couldn't sleep all night, waiting for breakfast."

Jim grabbed Dan's hand and helped him onto the shore and they walked back to camp where everybody was up and getting themselves ready for the day. Julie handed each of them a plate of fried eggs and bacon, "Enjoy, and if you eat everything on your plate you can have some baked beans for dessert."

Dan laughed, and Jim acted like what a treat it would be to have baked beans for dessert, which made Julie laugh. After breakfast was over and the camp was torn down, they readied themselves for the rest of the hike into the valley of the giants. Jim, taking the lead one more time with Julie next to him, was followed by the

Professor, Ann, Dan, and the Dean pulling up the rear, started down the trail. At this point it was all downhill for them and they made good time getting to the valley. Once there, Dan and Ann were impressed with what they saw as the valley opened up to them. Jim and the others pointed out things to both of them, showing where the tombs were and where the actual village was for the people that had once lived there. When they were ready to move on, Jim led them to their next camp site towards the face of one of the cliffs. Using the steps, they climbed up the face of the cliff, above the tombs, and made their camp.

By noon, everything was set up for the delivery of the creature and all were waiting patiently for the helicopter to show. In the meantime, Jim and the Professor took Dan and showed him the tombs of the other Indians, explaining what they could about what they were looking at. As they went from tomb to tomb Dan was impressed and amazed at what he saw, especially the size of the skeletons and the way they were dressed, and wished that he could take the remains back with him to study.

Jim, knowing Dan's thoughts, interjected, "Don't even think about taking any of the remains back. I've already asked and was very strongly told by Red Hawk that now is not the time."

"Trust me, we have all thought about doing the same thing," the Professor added.

Accepting Jim's answer as the final word, he then ask about the paintings on the walls of each tomb and why they were different. Jim told Dan that each painting basically told the story for each of the giants buried in the tomb. The paintings indicated the life and times of the individuals and of their exploits while living. After they had finished exploring the tombs, they headed back to camp for lunch and to wait for the helicopter to arrive.

After lunch Jim caught the sound of the chopper first. Looking up into the sky he and Dan climbed back down from the face of the cliff to meet the helicopter with its load. Waving their arms, the pilot and co-pilot caught sight of the two of them, and came in on top of them hovering, and then moving to the left of them set the container down onto the ground. Unhooking the load from the chopper, the helicopter lifted off into the sky and flew past the mountains till they were out of sight. By now, the Professor and the Dean were there to help unbuckle the container holding the creature. The girls watched from the cliff as the men did the work.

The creature was still heavily sedated for the flight and the men grabbed him by the arms and legs and half carried, half dragged him, to the first tomb. They were having a hard time doing this until Red Hawk and his friends showed up to help. Each of them grabbed an arm or leg, picking him up and carrying him to the cave. Laying the creature in his coffin, he laid there as if he were already dead. Dan and Jim were amazed at how easy it was for the four Indians to carry him to his tomb. After getting him inside the tomb, Dan looked around inside the cave, seeing the paintings on the walls of the tomb, he asked Jim, "What do they mean?" pointing at the drawings.

Jim looked at Red Hawk, "Ask him, he can tell you better than I can."

As they left the tomb, the four Indians put the wooden poles across the opening of the entrance so that the creature couldn't escape again. Red Hawk said, "Many moons ago there was a village in a valley, such as this one here, but in a different location. The creature you see there was one of many who would eat the flesh of their enemies, who were a peaceful loving people and who were nomadic in searching for their own food. They took care of these creatures until they were tired of doing so, by feeding them from their hunts. This one year the food was scarce and there was hardly enough for the tribe to eat, let alone the creatures. Feeding themselves first, there wasn't enough to go around for the creatures. This made the creatures mad and they decided to eat their Indian friends in order to survive. Of course, this did not bode well for the Indians at all. After having lost some of their people from the creatures eating them, they decided to kill the creatures to protect themselves. The creatures lived in a cave not far from the village and the Indians chased the creatures back to their cave. When the creatures refused to come out to fight, the Indians gathered wood and placed it at the front of the cave and started it on fire. The Indians would kill them one by one as the creatures tried to escape the fire. The ones that refused to come out and fight, died inside the cave from the smoke of the fire."

"This place wasn't called Lovelock, Nevada, was it?" Dan asked

"Yes, that is what they call it now. How do you know of this place?"

"He doesn't know what I do for a living does he?" Dan said, looking at Jim.

Jim explained to Red Hawk what Dan was doing for his research and development job. Red

Hawk looked at Dan, "I know you now, you were one of the ones who disturbed the ancient burial grounds of the giants, my ancestors."

Dan went on to explain that what they were doing was trying to find a way to use some of the genetics to save lives in combat through the healing process of the giants.

"You'll not be able to do this because it is not given for you to know and if you continue, it will destroy you and all of your people working on it with you," Red Hawk declared.

After saying his piece, Red Hawk walked away and as he left the cave he turned to Dan, "Remember what I said," and was gone, as if he had never been there.

"How do you know this?" Dan asked, as he was looking for Red Hawk.

"Trust him on this one, Dan. I don't know how to explain, but you just need to trust him on this." Jim said.

Dan didn't know what to say to either of them about the subject. But he knew that if Jim said so, it must be true. Dan just stood there for a moment, looking and feeling chastised by Red Hawk from his words. Walking away towards to the campsite, he climbed back up the face of the cliff and sat down next to the fire. Julie came over, "I know you don't understand all of what is going on here, but if Red Hawk says to stop, it isn't because he hates you it's because he cares for you."

"But, I don't understand what he means by it all."

"Sometimes you have to go by faith in order to find the truth in what you are searching for."

By now Dan was frustrated that all of the work he was responsible for was now for nothing, and that would mean he would be out of a job soon. It would be ten years of work and research with nothing to show for it. As he was contemplating all of this, the sky above the valley started turning to gray and lightning started flashing. The sky went from grey to turning dark, with thunder coming in from the south of the valley, bringing with it rain, which was starting to fall.

Red Hawk, looked at Jim, "Get to high ground with your friends and stay there until we come and get you. Whatever you do, don't leave the high ground, do you hear me?"

"I understand," said Jim, looking surprised by Red Hawk's words.

By now, the Dean and the Professor were quickly climbing up the steps with Jim following close behind them, getting there just in time to see the rain start to fall. The ground of the valley floor was starting to bubble up, and from their vantage point, all of them could see people coming up out of the ground, all of them were warriors, dressed for battle carrying shields and wearing breastplates to protect their vitals from serious injury during combat.

Jim, watching all of this, saw lightning strike the tomb of the creature, causing the logs across the opening of the tomb to splinter into kindling. The creature, as he lay in his coffin inside his tomb, opened his eyes and let out a scream. Sitting up in his coffin, he quickly jumped out. Coming out of his tomb, he was met by the others like him. The creature from the cave was in the lead, and as he howled, the lesser leaders formed behind him with their followers. These creatures had traveled from the north as a group, waiting for their leader to come forth from the tomb. The leader, having his sword in his hand, howled once more, this time other creatures appeared, dressed in just loin clothes, they started to form ranks as well.

Looking towards the north end of the valley, at first it looked as if the there were only a few of the creatures there but as they moved forward, more appeared behind the others. Their army was prepared, in that each of them carried swords and shields as well. There were others, not as big, forming ranks to the side of the giant creatures, who were the size of modern day man, who were carrying spears while others like them were carrying bows and arrows. They formed their ranks on the flanks of the creatures and went down the entire length of the army of creatures.

Dan couldn't believe his eyes, as all of this was occurring right before him. He only now started to realize the scene unfolding in front of him and the others. The spirits of the warriors inside the other tombs started flying out from their tombs and started lining up on the valley floor. Each of them had a sword in their hands, raising it towards the sky with lightning hitting their raised swords. As the ones coming from the earth started to form an army behind their leaders, some of them were carrying banners with different symbols on them. As the leaders took their place in line, the other warriors from the ground were running to find their places behind their respective leaders, each shouting their war cry once more.

Jim could see Red Hawk was the main leader of the warriors, with his sword raised in front of all the other leaders. Behind him he could see Running Bear, Grey Cloud, and Big Eagle, all standing in the front as leaders with their men coming to form around them. Each group had foot soldiers, each with shields and swords used for close quarters combat with the enemy, who formed the front line, and next were the archers behind them. Behind them were soldiers mounted on horses, waiting to break through once the foot soldiers cleared a path for them to fight. From the looks of it there must of have been thousands of soldiers ready and waiting to fight.

It was like watching the earth come alive for the first time and seeing what had happened many years ago. Jim pointed out to Julie and the others where Red Hawk was, along with his friends, who were the other leaders. Dan, again, couldn't believe what lay before him on the valley floor. Two great armies were now formed in columns, waiting for their leaders to sound the charge. The creatures were now formed, with some of them wearing head gear in the shape of skulls, and others were wearing helmets with horns sticking out of them like the Vikings used to wear, others had horns sticking out of the front of their helmets. Each creature stood at least twelve feet tall, some as tall as fifteen feet.

The wind had died down and the rain stopped with the ground once again solid and dry. As

Red Hawk looked down at his men, each of them standing with their swords in the air. He greeted each of his friends with a yell, signifying his approval of the army behind him. The infantry now locked their shields together and moved as one when they formed up. Each soldier was now ready to move forward into battle. Big Eagle raised his sword in the air, signifying his army was ready as well. As Red Hawk went down reviewing each column of soldiers he returned to the front of the army, sitting on his horse, he now faced the creatures, ready for battle. Next to Red Hawk was another soldier dressed as he was, but this person had blonde hair. Jim looked closer and realized it was Red Hawk's wife in battle dress ready to fight, as well. And as Jim looked closer at the other soldiers, he realized that there were women in all of the ranks.

Off to the side, where the cliffs formed, Jim and the others could see people watching from their own vantage point. These people were children and the old people who couldn't fight. Their job was to take care of the ones who couldn't join in the fight. Each of the old people were cheering their army on to victory. Looking above them, Jim could see other people who were the spiritual leaders praying in unison for their soldiers, and as they got up from their prayers they climbed down the face of the cliff and took their places in front of the army each riding a horse showing that the lord was on their side. As they formed up in front, the armies would shout in their language their approval of the religious leaders taking their place. When all were gathered to their rightful places, the army started moving towards the creatures, who in turn started moving towards the army themselves. Pretty soon the army was running towards the creatures, yelling in unison, so much so, the whole valley reverberated from the sounds of the war cry's.

By now, the spiritual leaders lowered their face shields and charged head long into the line of creatures, striking them with their swords as they went through their lines. The infantry stopped and opened ranks as did the archers in their middle, to allow the horse soldiers access to the front of the line, following the spiritual leaders and the captains into battle, creating an opening in the ranks of the creatures. Once the horse soldiers were through, the infantry and archers closed ranks and pushed ahead, helping to split the army of creatures into two groups. The first line of creatures fell from the onslaught of horsemen and fell to the ground, either dead or wounded. The archers fired upon the flanks of the creatures, their arrows darkening the sky as they sailed into their intended targets. The creatures who had shields, raised them in anticipation of the arrows hitting their targets. While the ones without shields were hit multiple times by the arrows. After firing their arrows, the archers formed onto the flanks of the foot soldiers and continued firing at the creatures as they moved forward with the foot soldiers.

Red Hawk had driven his horse into the main portion of the creatures, looking for the leader to kill him. Looking around, he found the creature fighting one of the spiritual leaders who had been in the lead. The creature's sword had killed the leaders horse and the leader was trapped under the body of the horse. Pinned and not able to move, the spiritual leader continued to fight off the attack of the creature until Red Hawk could get there. As the creature raised his sword to kill the leader, Red Hawk came by and cut off the creatures arm with his sword. This gave Red Hawk time to remove the spiritual leader from under his horse and get him away from the creature. The creature went back into the main portion of his army and waited for his arm to heal itself. Grabbing another sword, he continued to fight against the humans. Now the field of battle was covered with bodies from both sides and it looked like it could go either way. Red Hawk, sensing this, reorganized all of his forces under his leadership, with the second captains forming on him. The archers fell back into their own line, with the foot soldiers lining up as a unit in front of them, and the horse soldiers forming behind the archers, once more. This time, Red Hawk yelled to his men, "For our God and Country!"

The men all heard this, raised their swords in unison and started running towards the creatures once more. This scared the creatures who had lost more than they had planned. Their leader, sensing this, howled at them to stand their ground and fight. The ones who had started to run from the battle stopped, turned around, and charged back into the fight determined to destroy their enemy.

The archers now moved with precision as they picked their targets, with instinctive reflexes as they drew their bows and released their arrows, each one finding their target. This slowed the creatures down enough that the horse soldiers could find them and kill them with ease. The main brunt of the attack was being played out on the foot soldiers, who were not only dealing with the big creatures but also the smaller creatures, who were protecting their flanks. The horse soldiers kept coming in and taking out the bigger creatures with each charge. The archers were now looking for targets of opportunity to slow the advance of the creatures, especially the smaller ones that made up the flank. The tide of the battle started to turn on the third charge, with Red Hawk in the front leading the army again. The second captains, following Red Hawk, shouted encouragement to their soldiers as they led the charge.

The chief of the creatures realized that the battle was going bad for his side, howled once more, ordering retreat from the battlefield. Red Hawk, seeing this yelled, "The victory is ours, don't let them escape and take no prisoners!" The human army chased after the creatures from the valley, and as they came upon them, they killed them. By the end of the day all but one of the creatures had died. It took four men to tie the leader up and bring him back to the valley where Red Hawk was sitting on his horse watching the wounded being tended to as others searched among the dead for survivors.

As the leader of the creatures was brought before Red Hawk, he and his wife looked at the creature as he howled, knowing no one was coming to save him. Not knowing what to do, he gathered his second captains and religious leaders together to determine what to do with the creature. In the meantime, the creature was tied up and was being guarded by a dozen soldiers.

As the war council met together in the night the account of the war was told. Of all the men who had fought in the battle, only a thousand of them had fallen in battle. The other five thousand soldiers were either wounded or okay. The total number of the creatures killed was ten thousand. In the end there were no survivors of the creatures. Red Hawk listened to the body count as each second captain told of his men he had lost in battle. All were grieved in their losses but were happy that the valley was still theirs to live in. For the humans, it was an honorable fight to protect their homes and family and livelihood. In the days that followed, the living would bury the dead, both creature and human, and have funeral services for the human dead with a special day set up to honor their God for protecting them from the creatures.

Jim and the others had watched the battle play out below them and saw the human army start pushing the creatures out of the valley back up into the mountains. The thing that was really surprising to them was how ferocious the creatures were when it came to fighting against the humans. All of the humans that were wounded were killed immediately, no quarter was given by the creatures. In turn, the humans would push past the wounded creatures to fight the next one in line. Eventually, the humans would come off conquerors in the fight against the creatures. Their battle plan worked like it was supposed to. By splitting the army of the creatures, they were able to divide their forces and concentrate on the bigger threat by singling them out.

None of them, in all of their days, had ever seen anything like this kind of fighting before and were amazed at the ability of the humans to conquer the bigger creatures like they had done. Jim and the others hadn't realized that the battle they had been watching had been fought centuries earlier in another timeline. The place was correct, but for all of the army that was there, both sides had died years ago before the white man or the Indian had stepped foot in this valley.

Dan didn't know what to say or why he had to see all that he had seen going on in the battle. By now, he knew that Red Hawk had spoken the truth about the work he had been doing as useless, and he knew it would eventually kill all involved with it. The creatures, from his perspective, could not be considered human except in a physical sense. Their fierce spirit could not be controlled and to try and harness the healing qualities would be lost on the human race. Dan saw the carnage from the battle and it turned his stomach, he knew that from this point on he would need to change his job for something that would add to life, not to take it away.

Jim and Julie sat and looked at the battlefield as the humans looked for survivors, knowing there would be none, hoping that just maybe, they might find some. The other soldiers went about separating the bodies of the humans from the creatures for burial. The humans were carried back to their families and you could hear the crying of the women folk and their kindred when either their husband, father, and or brother was brought back to their place of living. The creatures were transported and buried on the north end of the valley. The bodies were stacked on top of each other and dirt was put in between the layers of bodies. Because of so many bodies there were quite a few mounds prepared for the dead creatures. The Professor and Ann stood there watching with Jim, Julie, and the Dean. All of them were quiet and really there wasn't anything to say at this point, for Jim the question that was on his mind was, "Why was it important for all of them to witness the battle in the valley? What was he and the others to learn from it?"

In an hour, the valley was back to normal and in real time for them. The mounds of the dead creatures were covered up by another sixty feet of dirt and rock. The valley was quiet, and the stars were all out, with the Milky Way showing off in the night. Jim and the others sat by the fire, deep in thought, thinking about all they had seen earlier in the day. None of them were hungry for any hot food and just snacked on whatever was available. Jim and Julie just sat sitting next to each other and were inseparable as if they were consoling each other. The Professor and Ann were the same, with the Professor's arm around Ann's shoulder and her head on his shoulder. Dan and the Dean were adding wood to the fire to keep it burning. They all sat by the fire, tired but not wanting to sleep. Eventually, Julie started dozing by the fire and Jim took her to the tent, crawled in next to her and went to sleep. The Professor and Ann were the next ones to retire for the night. Dan and the Dean were sitting by the fire and Dan had a stick he was using to play with the fire. Dan spoke to the Dean, "Why was it important for us to see the battle in the valley?"

"I don't know right off, except maybe for us to understand what war is all about. Maybe it's not a glorious thing as we are sometimes led to believe, and that war is something that we should use only as a last resort to protect our rights and country against all others that threaten our way of life."

Dan nodded at the thought that the Dean had put out, "I know one thing for sure, it isn't pretty or adventurous in any way shape or form. I know that war is sometimes required but only as a defense never as a pretense to start."

"I believe you're right in your understanding."

As they sat there looking at the fire, the Dean added, "For us scientists, we see archeology as a science that is impersonal and objective and all we see are the artifacts we find and from there we try to determine what happened to the people we're studying. Always looking for answers to the questions as to why they disappeared and how they lived and died. The biggest question about all of this is, how do their lives reflect on ours and what can we learn from them that will benefit us today?"

"My thought has always been about survival of the fittest in a combat situation for our troops. Is it better training or better technology that will save lives or is it just plain luck of the draw. I don't know if I believe that when it's your time to die then it's your time, no matter what you do you can't change it. From my point of view, it was my job to try to hedge our bets in order to save lives in combat, no matter the cost."

"There is a purpose to all things in our lives. Nothing is given without a reason for us to learn. Sometimes the death of one, by a so-called accident, is studied to save others from the same thing happening again. I don't believe in chance and I definitely don't believe in accidents. Things happen for a reason, sometimes we don't understand it. I believe it's up to us to learn from them, so we don't have to keep going over the same things twice or three times, in order to learn, otherwise how can we grow?" the Dean said.

"Do you really believe that, Dean?"

"I'm too old not to," he said, as he chuckled to himself."

Dan looked at the Dean, "I hope someday, I'm as smart as you are."

"Well I don't know if I'm smart, but I do believe I'm smart enough to know that I'm ready for bed right now."

"You go ahead Dean, I think I'll stay up a little longer," as he continued to play with his stick in the fire.

"Well in that case goodnight then."

"Goodnight Dean."

In about an hour, Dan stood up and looked back up into the night sky and saw a falling star and said to himself, "Star light, star bright, first falling star, I've seen tonight, Oh I wish I may, Oh I wish I might, I wish could have my wish tonight," and not saying anything more from that point on, he turned around and headed off to bed.

Being able to see the night sky once he was settled in for the night, he could see the stars again and, occasionally, he saw a satellite moving slowly across the sky. Dan wondered what it would be like to see the earth from the perspective of the satellite, as he slowly drifted off to sleep.

Chapter XV

The next morning the sunrise was majestic as it made its way over the mountain peaks. The air was clear and cool again for this time of the year. All of the team was still asleep and none of them were moving. They were comfortable in their sleeping bags and the early morning chill was enough for them to stay in their tents and sleeping bags a little longer. Julie was the first to move, and in so doing, Jim woke up, being comfortable and warm he stayed inside his sleeping bag. Seeing the sun was out already, he figured what the heck he was warm and no use being the first to get out of his warm confines. As he lay there in his warm sleeping bag he was able to see the sunrise continue over the mountains and into the valley from where he was.

The shadows across the valley were disappearing and the birds were singing in the valley below him. Remembering what he had seen the day before and seeing things now, was quite a contrast of perspective between yesterday and this morning. Jim was still thinking about why they had a firsthand account of the battle that was fought over thousands of years ago. What were they supposed to learn from all of this? By now, the others were coming around and starting to get up to start the day. Julie leaned over and kissed Jim as he lay there deep in thought, "A penny for your thoughts."

"It's more like a dollar for my thoughts this morning."

"Well, for what it's worth, good luck in them. Now that all of this is done, what do we do now?"

"I don't know, what do you think we should do? Maybe go home to our old boring jobs at the college?"

"I'm not sure either at this point, although that sounds good to me right now."

"Hey Professor, are you awake?" asked Jim.

"I am now, what do you want?"

"What should we do now that the creature is back in his tomb?"

"I think we should go and confirm that he's back in his tomb."

"I agree, whenever you're ready to go, let me know."

"Will do, how about we do breakfast first, before we go and look?"

"Depends if it's baked beans or not for breakfast."

Julie laughed and smacked Jim in the arm as he said that, "Just for that, you're getting a double helping now."

"Wow, look at the time, I don't know if we have time for breakfast."

After breakfast all of them decided to go check out the tombs on the first level. As they each climbed down the stairs they went together to look and see what they would find. As they went from cave to cave, each of the caves were now empty. There was nothing to even indicate that anybody had been there, no artifacts, no paintings no coffins nothing at all. Jim was really perplexed at this, as was the Professor and the Dean. Julie and Ann were also confused with what they had discovered. Walking to the other side of the valley, they checked inside those caves on the top and bottom levels as well. Finding nothing, to even hint that anybody had lived here today or a thousand years ago, was to say the least, confusing to all of them. Jim sat down on a tree stump and looked at the Professor, "Well what do you make of this Professor?"

"I don't know, I'm just as confused as you are about it."

"Maybe it didn't happen after all," the Dean said.

"Yeah, maybe we got a hold of some bad baked beans or something," Dan said smiling.

"If this is a figment of our imagination, how come all of us saw it then?" Ann asked.

"Maybe all that we experienced was for us to learn something from, as far as the battle went? Maybe it's about having faith and going by faith in what we saw and heard this whole time," Julie said.

"I don't know about this faith and the religious aspect of it. I think we're to learn different things about all of this. Maybe each lesson is unique to our own needs," Dan said.

"Maybe you're right on that Dan," the Professor said.

As they started walking back to their camp, they crossed the valley once more. As Jim was looking down, he saw an arrow sticking in a tree. Pulling it from the tree limb, he noticed a few more artifacts lying near the trunk of the tree. Picking them up, he showed the others what he had found. As the others started looking around on the ground, each of them found some kind of artifact nearby where they stood, as well. The Professor found a spear tip, Julie found a part of a bow, Ann found some arrowheads, Dan found the biggest artifact, a piece of buckler for a sword, and the Dean found part of a head dress. Each of them looking at what they found, now knew for certain that there had been a battle here in the valley.

Jim, looked around, "I guess this means were not going crazy after all."

"I believe you're right on that one. Maybe this is for us to remember that it was real after all," Dan said.

As they continued making their way back to the face of the cliff, they climbed the stairway up to where they were camped, and saw Red Hawk, Big Eagle, Running Bear, and Grey Cloud sitting by the campfire. Jim, looked at Red Hawk, "So did all of this happen that we saw yesterday?"

"What do you think, Jim?"

"I believe it did," said Julie.

"Me too," said Ann and Dan.

The others nodded in agreement at what their partners said. Red Cloud, looking at Jim, said, "What do you think, Jim?"

Jim stood there for a moment, thinking about everything that happened over the last two and half years and his fight to find the creature. He said out loud, "If it wasn't real, I'll be damned if I know what is real anymore."

Red hawk laughed, as did the other Indians. Jim finally accepted the fact that there are somethings that can't be explained by science and you just have to have faith in order to make sense of things sometimes. Believing is more important than seeing sometimes. Maybe that was the lesson for Jim, when it came to the battle between the creatures and humans. Julie could see the aha moment hit Jim after his comment. Reaching out to him she asked, "How do you feel?"

"I'm better now that I understand that faith is more important than fact," Jim said, as he looked at her.

Jim realized that the whole experience was for his own growth and for his understanding that things don't always add up to the logical answer, sometimes the solutions to questions are not always black and white. The creature was something that he took for granted and dealt with accordingly as he had in all things in his life. The truth was always nice and neat and tied with a pink ribbon and could be compartmentalized away inside his brain, pulled out when he needed to use it again. There was never any room for doubt in Jim's mind, however, that being said, the battle they had witnessed the day before, could not be explained by the artifacts that they had found. For the first time in his life he had to go by faith that what he saw was real.

For Dan, the lesson was about finding some meaning to his life instead of going through the motions and not knowing why. His growth came from dealing with something he couldn't explain away as a fact or figure. Life wasn't a bunch of X's and O's on a piece of paper. Life was about learning to adapt and modify when called upon to find the good in it and be happy with what you found. The battle showed what had happened centuries ago, but who would believe it even if he decided to tell someone about it. This realization couldn't be put in a letter, in triplicate, and submitted to the higher ups for evaluation for progress. He would have to be content knowing it had been for real even if no one else believed him. This was the same message as Jim's, but from a different perspective for Dan.

The Professor had learned from the battle as well, his came from finding someone else to love, that he also could be loved for who he was. Ann had been looking for it to, and yet didn't know it herself. The emotions of being involved in the creatures life and times was enough for her to realize that life was too short to be stuck in the proverbial hole in the wall. The battle showed them both that the war is not about winning and losing, it's about choosing life over death. Seeing the humans fight for their right to live in the valley was enough for them to fight for what they had found in each other. To quote an old Beatles song, "Love is all you need."

The Dean learned that his family was important, and he missed them all the more when he heard the kinfolk crying when they had found out about the loss of their loved ones in combat. He also saw the joy on the faces of the soldiers realizing they were still alive and able to go home once more.

Julie learned that life is no good without having someone to share it with. Seeing the women alongside their husbands, getting ready to fight, meant that they had found something worth fighting for, even if it meant their own lives. Going home together was what was important, and in itself, nothing else mattered in life.

Dan was right about the battle, in that each had learned a lesson, and each saw the battle from their own perspective, the lessons learned were suited just for their individual needs.

Jim looked at Red Hawk and the other Indians, "So where do we go from here?"

"Where would you like to go Jim? The world is yours to do and be whatever you want, it's really up to you," Red Hawk said, as he pointed to the valley below him.

As Jim and the others looked across the valley they saw the Indian city once more, with all the people moving about and talking to one another as they went about their ways. The people were happy and free to live their lives in peace. As Jim turned to look at Red Hawk he soon realized that Red Hawk and the others were gone. He smiled to himself, "It is up to me to be happy and free. It has always been my choice all along."

Chapter XVI

As they left the valley for the last time, Jim and the others stopped at the boulder looking over the valley, for one more look back. Each of them saw Red Hawk, Running Bear, Big Eagle, and Grey Cloud at the base of the hill waving at them.

"You're more than welcome back anytime you wish," Red Hawk said, as he waived

"Thank you, my brother!" Jim yelled.

They all heard Big Eagle say, "You know I'm hungry for some baked beans with pineapple. I'm sure going to miss not having them around to eat."

The other three Indians just laughed as they rode away. The team stood there watching and laughing, as the four Indians rode away on their horses back to the valley.

"Come on it's time to go home now," Jim said as he looked at Julie and the others.

Making their way back over the mountain took the rest of the day to get to where they had left their vehicles. When they got there, they notice that there was a ranger was checking their vehicles out to see who they belonged to.

"Can we help you sir?" Ann said, when she showed up.

"No, now that you're here. I was just curious who these vehicles belonged to is all."

"Well the car belongs to me and the truck belongs to one of them over there."

The ranger looked over at the others as they unloaded all of their gear into the back of the truck. "I'm glad you guys showed up when you did, I was getting ready to call a tow truck to come get them."

"So are we then, as well," Jim said, smiling.

"Thank you for watching out for us sir," Julie said, as she got into the truck.

"No problem, that's why they pay me the big bucks, ma'am."

The Professor got into the car with Ann, "We'll meet you in town to get cleaned up for the trip back home. Same place as the last time we were here?"

Jim nodded, yes, as he put the truck into gear and turning around on the dirt road headed his truck back to Salida.

Reaching the motel and getting rooms, they proceeded to get cleaned up and presentable with the new clothes they had bought to wear.

Finding a café for something to eat was next on their list of things to do. Ann and the Professor, after dinner, had decided between themselves to stay a couple more days in Colorado in order to get Ann's affairs squared away so she could move to Utah permanently.

For Ann, it was just putting in a two weeks' notice, the hard part would be selling her home. Fortunately, the housing market was good, and her house sold quickly. The Professor sold his house as well and combining it with the extra money from the sale of Ann's house, they bought a cabin on some land up in the mountains as a wedding gift to themselves. Being able to see the Utah County valley through the mountains was a sight to behold, especially at night.

Dan rode back with them to get his affairs in order as well, he also took some time off to go back to Montana to see if his favorite girl was still there. He gave a two weeks' notice and quit his job, with the recommendation that they stop the work they were doing on the genetic testing of the creatures. His replacement, William Lee, laughed at him and mocked him as he proceeded to continue his work on the skeletons. Having to sign a non-disclosure statement before leaving, Dan went back to Montana to live and found his old girlfriend and started dating her again.

Jim and Julie, with the Dean, stayed overnight before heading back to Utah, picking up their Jeep the next day to get ready for the new fall semester coming up. The drive back across Interstate 70 was uneventful. When reaching the Utah border all of them sighed a big sigh of relief and honked their horn, knowing they were home again. As they continued driving, all of them had mixed feelings about their last adventure in Colorado, trying to determine if it was finally over or would there be another dream coming.

Post Script

As William Lee finished his teleconference with his superiors in Washington D.C., he closed his computer laptop and sat back for a moment to collect his thoughts about the meeting that just concluded and breathe. He was pleased that his superiors were happy with his progress in finding the genetic codes from the blood samples they had from the live creature. All thanks to his predecessor who had located the creature in central Colorado. Having been able to break down the genetic code, he felt good for only have taken over in the last three months.

Dan's work had been very helpful in isolating the genes to start working on the application of the serum to be used on some volunteers from the military for actual testing. The subjects had to be clean, and of course young, for the experiment to be effective. Of course, this would begin in the near future, after all of the hurdles and red tape were cleared.

He got up from his desk and walked to the door of his office, down the corridor to the main lab where the creatures were in the giant test tubes. As he looked inside the room and saw the tubes with the creatures inside them, he looked them over, and all he could think of was the awards and citations he would receive for this work to save soldiers' lives in combat. The possibilities of upward mobility that were in his mind, were unimaginable to him. The respect and money for his services and the offers from other places would be humbling to say the least.

As he walked around the laboratory he checked in with each of the doctors as they did their work. Checking their records for any updates since the teleconference and making sure everything was working and was on time. He left the laboratory and walked into the adjoining room where the skeletons were located. Seeing that there was nothing out of place in this section, he checked the records of the scientists working on the skeletons, as well. In all of his work, he couldn't believe that these giant creatures lived, not only in America, but all over the world. In fact, every time he looked at one of these skeletons he was amazed at their size. It reminded him of the first day on the job when they showed him both rooms, he was literally speechless at what he saw. Now it had become somewhat normal, although he was in charge of it all. In his mind, he couldn't be too careful, and he knew being a good boss was to know what was going on all of the time.

Unknown to any of the people working inside the laboratory where the test tubes were located, the creature that was the largest they had in the tubes, had created a weakness in the tube that was holding him in place. At first, it was a small unseen crack that wasn't visible to any of the scientists in the room, but as the creature kept trying to escape from the tube he was in, the fatigue in the metal at the base of the tube was starting to take effect. The solution in the tank was starting to leak from the crack in the glass into the base of the tube. The base had all of the electrical wiring for the tube to monitor the creature's blood pressure, heart rate, and oxygen flow being fed into the air hose attached to the creature's face. The solution had filled the base just below the electrical connections. The loss of fluid inside the tank was refilled as it was lost, but not enough of a fluid loss to constitute a problem that required any attention. Besides, the night crew was supposed to monitor all of the equipment for any maintenance issues and clean the place at night. The solvent from the tank was just a couple of drops next to the tube base. Barely discernable to the naked eye, but there just the same.

As the creature kept pounding on the glass of the tube the crack got a little bigger and wider until the solution seeped through and touched the electrical components of the base, causing the creature to be electrocuted and bursting the glass on the tube, spilling the solution all over the floor of the laboratory. Which set off a chain reaction to the other tubes in the room. They exploded as well once the solution hit their bases.

The solutions from all of the tanks that exploded seeped down into the electrical wiring under the elevated floors, causing the wires to spark and start a fire. The oxygen tanks that were being used in the laboratory caught fire after they were knocked down by the blast, causing the control valves on the tanks to come off, exploding and acting like missiles, going off in all different directions, hitting the computers in the room and the gas lines in the walls, which were punctured by the flying debris. Once the fire hit the Freon gas it caused a secondary explosion ripping through the whole complex. In all, it took less than a minute for the explosions to set off the alarms in the building. Shutting down the power on everything they could, they started evacuating the people out of the complex. Most of the people who were working in the space tracking and missile warning areas were able to get out with minimum problems. The night crew working in the laboratory and the adjoining room were not so lucky. For only having a night shift on duty, most of them died in the fire, the ones that were able to escape had second degree burns all over their bodies, this was due to some of the chemicals used in the laboratory. The ones that were able to escape would have to be quarantined for their own good.

William Lee was at home when he got the message about the fire and explosion at the complex. Driving to the complex to look at the damage himself, he was amazed at how the fire was now bellowing out of the tunnel and all anybody could do was watch and wait for the fire to die out before going in to contain it. It would take two days before they could get a fire crew in there to get close enough to the big door leading into the actual complex. It would be a month before they could determine what caused the fire in the first place. Once it was found to have been started in the laboratory, William Lee was called to Washington to explain what had happened and where they would be going from here in their research. "Everything that we had, including the research was gone, having been destroyed in the fire and explosions. Basically, we would have to start all over again," William Lee said.

At this same meeting it was determined that with everything gone and plus the cost of rebuilding the complex, there wasn't enough funding to do a restart on the project. Although, not blamed him for the fire and the loss of ten years' worth of research, because he was in charge it was decided that Mr. Lee would be reassigned to another project somewhere in Ohio at Wright Patterson Air Force Base for AFIT (Air Force Institute of Technology) operated by the Air force. He would stay there until he retired in obscurity, never being what he envisioned of himself as a big man in the world of new technology for saving lives in combat.

Dan, hearing of the fire in the Cheyanne Mountain Complex, called a few of his old friends he still knew down in Colorado Springs, asking what had happened. The only thing he could get from them was that, in a section that was off limits to the military, a fire and explosion had occurred and basically burnt and gutted out the whole complex. Dan, as he sat listening over the phone, thought to himself that he needed to call Ann and the others and let them know what had happened at the complex.

Calling Ann in Utah to let her know about the fire, she was surprised by the information as well. As they continued talking over the phone, each of them thought out loud how lucky they had been by not being there. At the end of their conversation, each of them went to their spouses and told them the news about the fire and hugged them, thanking their lucky stars that they were where they were. Each of them would remember the words of Red Hawk as a gesture of love for them from that point on.

The Professor called and told Jim and Julie about the fire and how it destroyed the complex and that the all of the work was gone. Jim and Julie smiled, thankful that their good friends, Dan and Ann, were safe and sound and that Red Hawk was right about it coming to no good for anybody.

For Jim and Julie, the giants that lay in their tombs in the valley in Colorado would never be disturbed again and the secret to the valley would remain a secret until Red Hawk would determine the time and place for it to come forth. Only Jim, Julie, and the others would know what lay hidden in the valley of the giants and what they knew they would neither confirm or deny.

The End

The Valley of the Giants

Epilogue

Jim and Julie continued to work at Brigham Young University for the next ten years. Shortly after getting back to Provo, Julie went to the doctor to find out why she had been so tired and noxious. After running a few tests, Julie came home to let Jim know they were going to have a baby. During the summer they would go to different parts of Utah and Colorado, looking for places to do their scientific digs. Once they were old enough, the kids would go with them as they would work the digs for summer vacation fun. Their favorite place was the San Raphael Swell, just outside of Huntington, Utah.

The Professor and Ann were married in Provo the following month and she gave up her job in Colorado to be with the Professor. Ann is currently working on her Doctorate in Geology and is an assistant Professor at Brigham Young University. They would go with Jim and Julie when they could, on their summer digs.

The Dean was happy to be home with his family and continued working at Brigham Young University, taking off in the summers, with his wife, to work the digs with Jim and Julie, with their god children.

Dan quit his job and moved back to Montana to be closer to his parents and his future wife, who had been waiting for him to return. They have two children and are happily married, working as a police chief of campus police at Montana State University. Occasionally, as time permits, they get together with Jim, Julie, and the gang during their vacations.

For all of them, the adventure was over, and life would never be the same again for any of them. The battle they had witnessed had a profound effect on all of them and was the common thread throughout all of their lives. When they would get together at times, especially at the digs, Jim and Julie would tell Ann and Dan about their first encounter with Red Hawk and the other Indians, including the old medicine man they had found in the cave. They also talked about their experiences with Dr. Jones and his henchman and what ended up happening to them.

In fact, a few years later, the Professor, looking through one of his text books, found a picture of four Indians standing together. They were dressed in their war paint and buckskins for the photo, and had a strong resemblance to Red

Hawk, Big Eagle, Running Bear, and Grey Cloud. The Professor showed the picture to Jim and Julie and they all smiled at it, knowing, it may of have been them after all.

They never went back to the valley, except one time to show Jim and Julie's kids and tell them about an ancient battle that once took place there. As the kids listened, they thought it was neat that their parents and god parents would know so much about the valley and what had happened there. Showing them the artifacts they had found there, only added to the story that Jim and Julie told. At one point in their story, Jim and Julie claimed they saw the battle all over again. Closing their eyes and opening them again the battle was over and gone.

www.ingramcontent.com/pod-product-compliance
Lightning Source LLC
Chambersburg PA
CBHW030254200626
46816CB00002BA/643